BARKING UP THE WRONG TREE . . . ?

There was no mystery about Kimi's origin. She'd done some minor damage and irked an evidently harmless and eccentric dog hater. When she belonged to Elaine Walsh, she'd hardly been taken beyond the front walk, so she hadn't had much opportunity to enrage anyone. I was beginning to conclude that Kimi hadn't been anyone's intended victim. But I couldn't shake the sense that Kimi was somehow involved, that she knew something, had done something, or could tell me something. I didn't know what . . .

W9-DEZ-886

A BITE OF DEATH

SUSAN CONANT

BERKLEY PRIME CRIME, NEW YORK

A BITE OF DEATH

A Berkley Prime Crime Book / published by arrangement with the author

PRINTING HISTORY
Diamond edition / April 1991
Berkley Prime Crime edition / February 1994

The Penguin Putnam Inc. World Wide Web site address is http://www.penguinputnam.com

ISBN: 0-425-14542-5

Berkley Prime Crime Books are published by The Berkley Publishing Group, a member of Penguin Putnam Inc., 375 Hudson Street, New York, New York 10014.
The name BERKLEY PRIME CRIME and the BERKLEY PRIME CRIME design are trademarks belonging to Berkley Publishing Corporation.

PRINTED IN THE UNITED STATES OF AMERICA

10 9 8 7 6 5

A BITE
OF DEATH

With the exception of the Fishmonger and its proprietor, Dorothy Batchelder, who has kindly consented to a brief, anonymous guest appearance, all actual locations and institutions in this book are used fictitiously, and all characters are entirely imaginary.

Many thanks once again to James Dalsimer, M.D., and Joel Woolfson, D.V.M. Any errors in human and canine medical matters are entirely my own fault.

For expert instruction on the behavior of the Alaskan malamute, I am grateful to the great dog of my life, *prima inter pares,* Frostfield Arctic Natasha, C.D.

Chapter 1

I was writing a story about a woman who died and came back to life as her own dog. What triggered the plot was a dream, and what triggered the dream was an article in the *Boston Globe* about a madman in Montreal who went berserk and shot thirteen women because he believed that feminists had ruined his life.

I hadn't got far with my story because the dream was about the woman, not the dog, and I was more interested in him than in her. When the woman came back, did the dog have to leave? Or did they coexist? I liked that better. But, with the former owner dead, at least superficially, who owned the two of them? Someone had to. I couldn't leave them to roam the streets, defending themselves against marauding canine bullies, nosing through trash cans for maggot-ridden bits of bony fish and splintery chicken legs, curling up in the cold with their one black nose tucked under their one plumy white tail for warmth—they were an Alaskan malamute—and with no one to remember their heartworm medication or make sure their shots were up to date. Even in fiction, you see, a dog is inevitably my responsibility. I was the one who'd dreamed up this one, and I couldn't leave him—or her?—alone with no one but a recently deceased, internal, invisible, and hence probably self-preoccupied and irresponsible owner.

Well, suppose it happened to me and mine: If I died and came back to life as my own dog, Rowdy, who should own us? Who better than myself? I am, in most respects, the perfect dog owner, and once I'd been reborn inside Rowdy's furry double coat and stubborn mind, we'd be the perfect dog as well. We'd have a head start on canine perfection: we'd already be an Alaskan malamute. And after my reincarnation, we'd have it made. For one thing, we'd henceforth come instantly when I called us. We'd quit stealing the sugar bowl from the kitchen table, licking it clean, and hiding it under the bedroom radiator. Our off-leash heeling would abruptly improve. We'd never lag on even the most sudden about-turn, and we'd look up at my face as if we were a dutiful golden retriever instead of the independent sled dog we knew ourselves to be. The three of us would make the perfect team, Rowdy and both of me.

Really, though, the two of us, Rowdy and I, weren't so bad as we were, or, depending on how you count, the four of us. Rowdy. Me. The part of him that lives in me. The part of me that lives in him. That's what having a dog is all about. It's risking death. Give him your soul, and you die a little. Then you come back to life as your own dog. And it works both ways, which may explain why I'm only half human. I've given my soul to dozens of dogs, and they've all come back to life as me.

It's a permanent situation that I didn't choose, although I would certainly have picked it if I'd been offered a choice. I never feel crowded, and I'm not allergic. I'm used to it. After all, it started *in utero,* or maybe even earlier, if you count the years before my conception, because my parents had been raising and training golden retrievers for a long time before it occurred to them to produce a litter that couldn't be registered with the American Kennel Club. Or maybe they thought mine could. Or maybe they planned to slip my registration form in with the ones for the two litters of goldens whelped just before me. It is even possible that they succeeded. I've never checked the golden retriever stud book for my own registration. Perhaps I'm there, Holly Winter, sired by Buck *ex* Marissa Winter, bitch.

If you're new to dogdom, you might assume that in calling me a bitch, Buck and Marissa and the American Kennel Club would have been issuing a rude comment on my character, but that's not the case at all. For one thing, in the world of purebred dogs, *bitch* is a good clean word for female, and for another thing, the only bad name my parents ever called me was the one they gave me. The American Kennel Club has never had any reason to bad-mouth me, either. I don't handle my own dogs in breed anymore—that's conformation, the part of a dog show that's about looks, not behavior—but I've always shown in obedience. I still do. When I had goldens, we did well. And Rowdy? Since no one expects anything of an Alaskan malamute in obedience except maybe some big laughs, I'm as proud of putting a C.D. on him as I've been of putting U.D.'s on golden retrievers. C.D. and U.D. are obedience titles, of course. C.D. is Companion Dog. That's like a high school diploma. C.D.X., Companion Dog Excellent, is college. Utility Dog, U.D., is a Ph.D., except that it takes more time, work, and brains. For instance, in Cambridge, Massachusetts, where I live, there are thousands of Ph.D.'s and practically no U.D.'s. That's why Cambridge is such a weird place. It has too many overeducated people and too many undereducated dogs.

But I've digressed. As I was saying, instead of finishing my regular column for *Dog's Life* magazine, I was writing a story about a woman who died and came back as her own dog. The column was giving me trouble because it was about how to introduce a second dog into the household. The source of the trouble was an unshakable fear that Rowdy, who was asleep at my feet under the kitchen table, would read either my handwriting or my mind. If I'd transmitted the thought that I might die and come back to life as him, he wouldn't have objected at all, but the possibility of having to share his favorite sleeping spots, his owner's attention, and, God forbid, his food and water dishes with another dog would have brought his hackles up. And he'd almost certainly have realized that what I had in mind was not just any other dog, but another malamute.

I went back to the story. Just as the woman was exhaling her last human breath, the phone interrupted me. The caller was Steve Delaney, Rowdy's vet and my lover.

"Holly, you busy?"

"I'm writing," I said.

"I need a favor. It's an emergency, I guess you'd say." He laughed a little. "I'd go, but I can't. I'm an hour behind schedule, and the waiting room's full. You can handle this better, anyway—it's a behavior thing. A client's stuck on her kitchen table. That's where she called from. She's got a malamute bitch that won't let her get off the table. She didn't know who else to call."

"Her first malamute, right?"

"Right."

"Is this a puppy?"

"Not exactly, but young. Anyway, she hasn't had her very long. And it's her first dog."

Getting a malamute as your first dog is like playing your first-ever basketball game as the Celtics entire starting five during a Pistons' home game. If you knew what you were doing, you wouldn't be doing it. A realistic aim is survival, not victory.

"Okay. So where does she live?"

"Upland Road." He gave me the number. "That's at your end of Upland, not the Mass. Ave. end."

That part of Upland Road isn't far from my house, which is the three-story red triple-decker at the corner of Appleton Street and Concord Avenue, across Concord from the new Observatory Hill town houses that Harvard built as affordable faculty housing. The town houses range in price from $185,000 to $300,000. An assistant professor makes maybe $30,000 a year. There you have the relationship between Harvard and reality.

"How am I supposed to get in if she can't get off the table?" I asked Steve.

"She says there's a key in the milk box. Under the empty bottles. Stupid place to hide a key."

Actually, that was where I used to leave mine before I had a milkman, which is to say, before I discovered that one of the luxuries Cambridge offers is the privilege of having milk delivered in real glass bottles that remind you of the kind your grandmother should have had instead of the waxy cartons and polluting plastic she did have. People always ask if the cream floats on the top, but it doesn't. It's plain old homogenized milk, but the eggs honestly are fresh, and the ice cream is pretty good, too.

"I hate to rush you," Steve said, "but could you get over there soon? The bitch won't hurt her, but she doesn't know that. Her name's Elaine Walsh. The woman."

"There aren't a lot of dogs named Elaine Walsh."

He liked that. "The malamute's called, let's see, Kimi. She's about a year old. Real pretty. Very dominant. That's the problem. And she's a big bitch, for this part of the country."

At a mere seventy to ninety pounds, the malamutes from the original New England strain—Kotzebues, they're called—are lapdogs compared with the hundred-and-thirty-pound mals you find elsewhere.

"Is this the first time it's happened?" I asked.

"First time she's called me. But, like I said, she hasn't had the bitch very long. It's complicated. It's a long story. I'll tell you about it later. Maybe she will. I've got to run."

"I'm leaving now."

"Good luck," he said. "Hey, thanks a lot. I'll see you tonight?"

"Sure," I said. "If there's anything left of me."

I was kidding. I'm not afraid of dogs.

Chapter 2

ELAINE Walsh's house had originally been a working-class triple-decker something like mine, the kind of house that my mother always disparaged as a tenement and that costs about $40,000 anywhere else and more than $100,000 in Cambridge—even before it's been renovated the way hers had. Some architect had covered the façade with vertical strips of wood painted a pale Brattle Street yellow, screened in the front porch with the same strips, and divided the porch in half to make separate entrances and create the illusion that the building wasn't one house but two. When people in normal places say "my house," they mean just that, a whole house, but in Cambridge, they're apt to mean half a house or even a third or a fourth of a house. All that distinguishes these fractional houses from condominiums is separate entrances, like the one to Elaine Walsh's.

The sidewalk in front and the short brick path that led to Elaine Walsh's entrance were covered with a thick coating of Halite that was melting the ice left by last night's sleet and ruining the soil in the railroad-tie beds of blackened marigold stalks on both sides of the brick. In an unintended effort to repair the salt damage, a large dog had made repeated applications of natural fertilizer.

Inside the vertical-strip porch, to the left of the door, sat an insulated sheet-metal milk box just like the one at my back steps, a mottled dull gray box with a schematic picture of a blue cow and "Pleasant Valley Farms" also painted in blue. Inside were two sluiced-out one-quart glass milk bottles, and under one was a key. In case Elaine Walsh had liberated herself, I rang the doorbell, but no one answered, and I let myself into a little entrance hall with a bentwood coatrack and a flight of stairs leading up.

A series of low snarls greeted me.

"Hello?" I called up the stairway. "Dr. Delaney sent me. Elaine? Miss Walsh? Are you okay?"

"For God's sake, I thought you'd never get here. And it's 'Elaine' or 'Doctor,' not that damned 'Miss.' "

I guessed right away she wasn't a real doctor. Have you ever heard an M.D. give you a choice about what to call her? Besides, Cambridge is Cambridge. Most of the people called Doctor are only Ph.D.'s, and at least half of the M.D.'s are psychiatrists, anyway, which usually means that they never wanted to go to medical school in the first place and forgot everything they learned there as soon as they graduated. Of course, we do have a few real doctors, like Steve, who was my lover before he was Rowdy's vet. We met just after he took over from old Dr. Draper, when my last golden, Vinnie, was finally feeling more pain than she or I could endure. Steve stopped her pain. I've missed her and adored him ever since. And if you're sleeping with your vet, you get to use his first name.

I unzipped my parka, shoved my gloves into one pocket, and extracted from another some of the tools of my trade: a metal training collar, a thin leather leash, and a small plastic squirt bottle filled with water. I primed the squirt bottle with a couple of squeezes.

The stairs led me to a big, beautiful open room with a high-ceilinged living area ahead of me and a kitchen area to my left. Sitting in a cross-legged yoga posture on a butcher-block table was a strong-looking woman in her early thirties. She had short black hair and the kind of rugged, weathered face you expect on an archaeologist. I wondered whether she was one. In Cambridge, it's hard to tell. The Moroccan rugs on the floor, the African masks on the off-white walls, the Hopi pots displayed here and there, and the rough-woven Greek-peasant shirt she wore weren't necessarily clues to her occupation. Ethnic never goes out of style here. Neither do pale-painted walls. The locally educated inhabitants of Cambridge favor a decorative approach to cultural pluralism: touches of multicolored exotica against an all-white background. It's a preference they learned in school. For instance, three of Harvard's sixty-one tenured law professors are African-American.

Anyway, maintaining that asana there on her kitchen table,
Elaine Walsh looked Caucasian with ethnic aspirations and
failed dignity, but her malamute looked congenitally Alaskan,
and not at all silly until she quit growling at Elaine Walsh, ran
over to me, hurled herself onto the floor, and presented me with
a furry underbelly to rub. Rowdy greeted most visitors with
the same display of suspicious reserve.

Elaine Walsh gave a big sigh, but stayed on her perch. "God,
this is humiliating."

The legs of the table and the legs of the wooden stools around
it showed the marks of a dog's teeth.

"You're not the first person it's happened to," I said.

While the malamute remained spread out on the floor, I
knelt down, slipped the metal training collar over the big, furry
head, and attached the leash.

"You can get down now," I said to Elaine. "She's leashed."
I rubbed the mal's tummy.

"I feel like such a dope." Elaine uncrossed her legs and
climbed down from the table. Although she must have been
marooned there for quite a while, she didn't move stiffly.
Maybe she really had been practicing yoga. "Thank you so
much. This is the dumbest thing that's ever happened to me.
I don't know what I would've done."

"You probably would've worked it out. She doesn't exactly
look vicious. Kimi, right?"

Elaine nodded and threw the mal a glance of wry, forgiving
disgust.

"She's pretty," I said. "She's just beautiful."

Like Rowdy and all other malamutes, she looked like a low,
heavy-boned, sturdy wolf with large, gentle dark brown eyes.
Rowdy, though, had a completely white face—an open face,
it's called—and she had what's known as a full mask: a caplike
patch of black on her head, a black streak down her muzzle,
and, around her eyes, a Lone Ranger mask that gave her a
slightly forbidding look. Her underbelly and the underside of
her tail were white but in need of a shampoo. When she rolled
over and stood up, I could see that the fur on her back and
sides was darker than Rowdy's, the color that's called dark
wolf gray, with traces of pale brown near her big wedge ears
and on her legs. Having risen to her feet, Kimi shook herself
powerfully all over, opened her jaws to reveal a set of menacing

teeth, and gave a series of ferocious growls, roars, and snarls. She wasn't merely expressing herself; she was fervently talking to *me*.

"Oh, no." Elaine backed away. "Here she goes again. Be careful. Do you know what you're doing?"

Kimi turned to her and issued another deep, throaty snarl.

"She's asking to go out," I said. "I'll take her. Kimi, come on. Let's go." I headed for the stairs with Kimi prancing after me, silent, tail wagging. Unlike wolves, malamutes carry their tails high over their backs. Kimi relieved herself on the dead marigolds, and I led her back in and up the stairs.

"She needed to go out," I said. "For malamutes, that's normal. Mine does it, too."

"She needed to go out," Elaine repeated with incredulity. "Well, that's not what she meant before. Believe me."

"She's your first dog, right? How long have you had her?"

"A month, and, believe me, it's been the longest month of my life. It seems like forever. Anyway, that's not just because of her. It has to do with her, but it's not all her fault. It's a long story. Do you think she's all right now?"

Kimi was standing stiff-legged at the end of the leash, her ears flattened against her head. She was turning her big soft eyes on Elaine and gently waving her fluffy gray and white tail. As any dog person would have known, she'd practically forgotten her own misbehavior and was imploring Elaine to do the same.

"She's fine. This is a submissive posture," I said. "Look, do you intend to keep her? Do you want to?"

Elaine leaned against the table. "It's complicated. That's part of the story. I more or less have to. And a lot of the time, she's fine. And then she'll turn like that. And she's just hell with other dogs. I can't even walk her. She attacks other dogs. But I don't know. This may sound crazy right now, but I like her. So the answer to your question is basically yes. I want to keep her. I must be out of my mind."

"Make me some tea," I said. "Let's talk. My name is Holly Winter. I train dogs. I have a malamute."

"God. I never even asked your name. I'm sorry."

I liked her for not smirking at my name. My parents, by the way, didn't intend it to sound funny. The bitches in the other two litters all had names like Winterland's Christmas Cookie

and Winterland's Sweet Noel; obviously, we were whelped in
December. Buck and Marissa didn't want me to grow up feeling different or inferior, which meant to them, of course, different from or inferior to a golden retriever. I also liked Elaine
for apologizing, and I liked her for wanting to keep a dog that
had chewed the legs of her furniture and driven her to take refuge on a tabletop. Of course, I adored Kimi, who was exactly
what I had in mind when I was trying to write that column
and hoping Rowdy couldn't read my thoughts.

Having calmed down enough to recover her manners, Elaine
took my parka, made a pot of Earl Grey, and insisted on building one of those pathetic little city fires (I'm from Maine) in
a free-standing metal mock fireplace that sat on a tile hearth
in the living area. When she put the teapot and cups on the
coffee table, I started to take a seat at one end of the gray-and-
white-striped couch that faced the fireplace, but Elaine stopped
me.

"That's Kimi's place." She smiled apologetically. "She
doesn't appreciate it if other people sit there."

It was Elaine's house. And Elaine's dog. I sat in the middle
of the couch, with Kimi still on the leash. She was sniffing at
the pitcher of milk on the coffee table. I almost expected Elaine
to let her drink it. And then, honest to God, Elaine did. Spatter-
ing milk all over the table, Kimi emptied the little jug and
licked it off without a single word from Elaine.

"I'll get some more," Elaine said. "Don't worry. I'll wash
the pitcher first."

As if I'd have cared. Better after a dog than after a person,
as my parents always said.

As soon as she returned, Kimi threw her a questioning look
and then leapt onto what she'd evidently claimed as her end
of the couch, right next to me.

"Don't move any closer to her," said Elaine, frowning at me.
"She'll snap at you. She's tough." Admiration filled her voice.

"I've gathered," I said. *You're not,* I wanted to add. *But
you're going to be.* "So tell me about her."

Once again, like Steve, she warned me that it was a long
story, but it wasn't.

"I'm a clinical psychologist," she said. "I teach, and I have
a private practice. I have an office on Mass. Ave. Anyway, a
month ago, I lost a patient, a young woman. It was the first

time that'd ever happened to me. I knew it was a terrible thing, when that happens. When a patient suicides. Or I thought I knew how hard it was. But I didn't. I can't describe it to you. It's something beyond terrible." Her face softened, and I realized that some of the weathered-looking lines around her eyes were recent.

"Kimi was her dog," I said quietly.

"Yes. My patient overdosed." On cocaine, I assumed, or something like that, mostly because *overdosed* always reminds me of Len Bias, who would've been the Celtics next Larry Bird if he'd celebrated less intensely than he did. "She left a note," Elaine continued. "They usually do, you know. It doesn't make it easier. This note was for me. She asked me to take her dog."

I edged about one inch toward Kimi, who glared at me and growled. I wrapped both hands tightly around her muzzle, gave her head a gentle shake, and said, "Kimi, cut that out." She did.

Elaine looked displeased.

"So she was willed to me." Elaine held her hands out, palms up, helpless. "And I'd never lost a patient before. It was as if my patient had said, 'Well, you didn't take care of me, and nobody else ever did, either. Here's your last chance.' And, of course, I'd never had a dog before. I had no idea what I was in for. It was the only thing left I could do for her, for my patient. She'd had a rough time, believe me. And we were just getting started, really. I'd heard about the dog, of course, and I'd pretty much thought the dog was something she had going for her. Or could have. There were problems there, too, of course."

"Big problems?"

"We're talking about a person who basically had problems everywhere, in every relationship. She'd been used. Victimized. She was depressed. She had a lot of anxiety. But the point is, I didn't see the dog as a problem dog."

"I think you were right," I said. "Some of this is an adjustment problem."

"Actually, I'm not so sure. I think maybe there's something wrong with her." Elaine looked embarrassed. "Maybe something hormonal."

"Thyroid?" Kimi's coat looked thick and shiny, and she

wasn't trying to get near the fire. Heat-seeking is one sign of hypothyroidism in dogs. "What . . . ?"

"This may sound kind of funny, but she lifts her leg," Elaine said. "Like a male dog. She doesn't always do it, but sometimes she does. On trees, fire hydrants. Not all the time, but a lot."

"She's a malamute," I said. "Hasn't anyone told you about them?"

"This is my first dog," she said sharply.

"Well, malamutes aren't quite like other dogs. For one thing, you'll find a lot of malamute bitches that are just as dominant as the dogs. As the males. That's why she lifts her leg. That has to do with dominance. It doesn't mean there's anything wrong with her. Lots of bitches do it, not just malamutes."

Elaine's face lit up. Her eyes gleamed just the way Kimi's had when she'd eyed the milk pitcher.

"In wolf packs," I added, "the leader is sometimes female, or a few reports say that, anyway. All dogs are descended from wolves, you know, but these Arctic breeds really show it. Just look at her. She looks like a wolf redesigned to haul a sled. And what that means is that they're very, very interested in where they belong in the pack. They need to know who's top dog. Dominance is why she lifts her leg, and that's why she drove you onto that table. Once she knows you're in charge, she'll be a lot easier. She isn't abnormal, and she isn't vicious."

I didn't anticipate the effect my little basic-dog-facts lecture would produce. Elaine cocked her head to one side like the old RCA dog hearing his master's voice on the Gramophone. "You want to hear something funny? You know what I do?" She eyed Kimi with delighted kinship. "You won't believe it. I give workshops for women. On assertiveness."

We both laughed.

She continued. "I actually wrote a book on women and power. I can't believe . . ."

I could believe it. In the canine cosmology of my parents, the natural order of the universe endlessly asserts itself in the matching of dogs and owners, but Elaine wouldn't have understood. "What a strange coincidence," I said heretically. "So really, you've probably ended up with the perfect dog for you. And you know? Obviously, you needed a dog. I mean, one thing I've never understood about the women's movement is how we're supposed to be strong all by ourselves. It's impossible."

She sat up straight, and her body tensed.

I went on. "I mean, a lot of this physical equality, self-sufficiency stuff is just bull. I'm young and I'm strong, but I could pump iron forever and not be able to bench-press half what a man can if he works out a little once a week. Right?"

"Many women have not had that experience," she said stiffly.

"The point is that it doesn't matter. Why should I do it at all? Unless I happen to get off on it, which I don't. If I want muscle, why not just get a big dog?"

"As a male substitute?" Elaine's eyes flashed. She and Kimi were an exception to my personal rule that dogs and their owners don't look alike. Muscular and compact, with their dark brown eyes and those black caps on their heads, they made a handsome brace, a matched pair, vital and spirited.

"No," I said. "Not at all. That's just psychoanalytic crap. Or feminist crap. You want to be free to walk anywhere you want, anytime you want? You think you can do that by pumping iron and holding rallies? Forget it. Get a big dog. Train it. That's real liberation. Or it's my kind."

"What a bizarre theory."

"And I'll tell you another thing." I was talking about something I believe in. "If you want a lesson in power and control, take up dog training. You know what happens if you're afraid of asserting yourself? If you don't insist that you're the one who's in charge? The dog runs all over you. It runs your life."

"So what?" she said. "Who cares? Power over dogs?"

"It's more than that, because one of the things you learn is to make things happen the way you want, even if the other guy is bigger and stronger than you are, whether the other guy is a dog or a person. I promise you, once you can order around a Great Dane or Doberman or an Alaskan malamute, you know your own strength, and a person is going to have a hard time intimidating you. Especially when the dog's with you, of course."

"Canine feminism," she said. "Has it ever occurred to you that putting a dog at the center of your life isn't all that different from putting a man there? It has the same effect, doesn't it? You're always second, aren't you? The dog is first. Or the man."

"Only if you grovel. What happens then is that you end up spending the rest of your life marooned in the kitchen."

"On the kitchen table. Okay." She smiled.

"Yes." I smiled back. "And seriously, that's not good for Kimi. She really does need to know where she belongs in your pack. What she needs to know is that you're top dog. That's what's behind most of this behavior. She isn't comfortable. Once you let her know that you're in charge, she'll relax and behave herself, and you'll have a great dog. You have a terrific future together."

Chapter 3

BEFORE I left, I presented Elaine with the squirt bottle and instructions about using it. The next time Kimi snapped at her or tried to drive her onto a tabletop, Elaine was supposed to say no firmly and quietly, and give her a couple of blasts of cold water right in the face. If you don't misuse or overuse a squirt bottle, it works like magic.

We met again the next day and the two days after that. My goal wasn't so much to teach Elaine to train Kimi as to help her have enough control to take Kimi to the Cambridge Dog Training Club, where Vince, our head trainer, could take over. On my first return visit, I gave Elaine a lesson on how to use a training collar, otherwise known as a choke collar or choke chain. Kimi was so wild that Elaine had stopped trying to walk her, and the lack of exercise was making Kimi wilder than ever. On my second return visit, we went around the block. I walked Kimi a little, and Kimi dragged Elaine. Malamutes are Arctic bulldozers, and you need a training collar to control that tremendous strength, but Elaine hated the collar, even after I showed her how to jerk it to knock Kimi off balance, not to choke her. I'm no psychologist or therapist, but even I could tell that Elaine wasn't scared of hurting Kimi. What frightened her was power, Kimi's and her own.

"Counterphobic," Rita said later. "Hence the book. Women and power." Rita's my second-floor tenant, my friend, and a therapist. Not *my* therapist. Dogs are my only healers.

Each day after the training, Elaine and I had tea. The first time, Elaine put out a plate of cookies and stood by while Kimi ate them all. The second day, before we sat down, I asked Elaine to take Kimi's place on the couch. At first, she refused, but I didn't back down. When Kimi growled at her, she aimed the squirt bottle at her black mask, squeezed, and yelled "No." Then she put the bottle on the coffee table. Kimi already knew what it was. Elaine and I got to eat the cookies that day.

And we talked. She knew Rita. They'd been in a supervision group together, which is apparently equivalent to the seminars that instructors like Vince attend, training about training. In fact, something became clear to me that I'd already half suspected from listening to Rita, namely, that psychotherapy is a misguided form of dog training, and the reason therapy takes so long and seems so complicated is that it's missing the key ingredient: the dog. Elaine didn't agree. Neither does Rita.

We also talked and talked about women's issues. She said that when women write, we don't write as women because language is male. I said that I did and mine wasn't, but she was unimpressed, mainly, I suspect, because dog writing isn't taken as seriously as it should be, especially by feminists, probably because of Jack London. When I said that Virginia Woolf was principally a dog writer, Elaine got really furious, even though I'd meant it as a compliment to Virginia Woolf, but we both admired *Flush,* which, in case you didn't know, is Virginia Woolf's biography of Elizabeth Barrett Browning's cocker spaniel and the world's first feminist dog story.

Elaine thought all marriage was slavery. When I thought about who should stay at my side, I said, I was deciding between a malamute and a golden retriever. Or possibly an Akita. She called me frivolous. I called her grim. My dogs, according to Elaine, kept me locked into fulfilling the needs of others. They impeded my freedom. I said that love and work always do. We argued about violent oppression and gentle protection. She gave me a copy of *Writing a Woman's Life,* by Carolyn Heilbrun. I gave her a copy of *How to Be Your Dog's Best Friend,* by the Monks of New Skete.

A few days after my last visit, soon after our friendship began, my friend Elaine Walsh died. I wish someone had broken the news to me, but no one knew to call me, I guess. I found out about her death from the *Boston Globe.* It was also from the *Globe* that I learned that Elaine had been almost famous, at least in Boston and Cambridge.

"A well-known feminist psychotherapist," the *Globe* called Elaine. In addition to the book on women and power, which

I already knew about, she'd written a couple of others. I'd never heard of them. They probably weren't about dogs. The paper quoted a professor who called the books "seminal" and "revolutionary" and also said that Elaine had been the victim of the same violent oppression she had devoted her life to battling. Elaine's death, according to the professor, showed that the struggle for women's rights was truly a struggle for women's lives. The *Globe* quoted that professor, but didn't come right out and announce that Elaine had been murdered. It said that she'd been found dead and that the police were investigating. If she'd died a natural death, the paper wouldn't have put in that quote, but the whole account was vague and inadequate. For example, the *Globe* didn't even mention Kimi.

My first thought, of course, was of Kimi, not that she'd finally behaved so badly that she'd driven Elaine to suicide, but that she might be dead, too. That my first thought was of Elaine's dog may strike you as hard-hearted, but I won't apologize. If I'm ever found dead, I hope there'll be people whose first thought is of my dogs. With a father like mine, of course, I don't need to worry. "Damned shame," he'll say as he packs my dogs into his van. "Damned shame. She was a nice bitch."

"Kevin? Holly. I have to ask you about something."

Kevin Dennehy is my next-door neighbor on Appleton Street, but I'd reached him at the Central Square Police Station, where he works.

"If this is about a lost dog," he said, "I don't have time. You know why I don't have time? Because I just got a big promotion."

"Congratulations, Kevin! I didn't know you'd applied."

"Yeah," he said. "I just got promoted. From animal control to homicide."

"I hate to be the one to break the news, Kevin, but that wasn't a promotion. It was a demotion. Anyway, this is partly about a person. And, uh, it's serious. Her name was Elaine Walsh."

"Right."

"I know it's right. She was a friend of mine. I want to know where her dog is."

"Holly, for God's sake."

"Is the dog all right?"

"Yeah."

"Good. That's great." I paused. "And where is she?"

"You don't want to hear about it." He had a macho-protective tone in his voice.

"Why not?"

"You have a hard time with death. Remember? You told me all about it. When you were a kid, your parents kept making you go to the funerals of all the family dogs, and you can't handle it, right?"

It wasn't so much the funerals as the deaths. Dogs have short life spans. We had a lot of dogs and a lot of death. Anyway, Kevin is in no position to criticize me for not being able to handle it. He doesn't have a dog because he was so broken up when Trapper, his last dog, died that he won't get another.

"So," he added, "you don't want to know the details. It wasn't a natural death . . ."

"I thought you said she was all right!"

"Hell, the *dog's* all right."

"Well, that's what I called about. One of the things, anyway. Where is she? Elaine's malamute, Kimi. I was helping Elaine with her, and now I want to know what you did with her. I know where Elaine is."

"Started out with Pat Shanahan, but he tied her to a desk, and next thing you know, she's dragged it ten feet and eaten a pizza the guys brought in, and they made Pat pay for it, and he got mad at the dog."

"What did he expect? She's a malamute. Born to pull. So where is she now? In the pound?"

"Yeah."

"I want her. Elaine left her to me." That was true. In spirit. Or would have been if Elaine had thought of it. "How do I bail her out?"

He told me and then said he had to run.

"Yeah. One last thing," I said. "How did Elaine die?"

"Looks like an overdose."

"Of cocaine?"

"Was she a regular user?"

"Not that I know of. I don't think so. Maybe I was thinking about Len Bias. Is that what she died of?"

"Doubtful," Kevin said. "So far, it looks like sleeping pills. That's a guess. Possibly suicide."

"But you don't believe that?"

"What we've got here is a lady who writes books, right? Gives talks. She's a lady you can't shut up. A feminist." Elaine would have loved that definition. Or maybe not. Kevin went on. "And here she is, ready to take what you might want to call a major step, right? And you're telling me she's got nothing to say about it? No note. Not a word."

"Yeah. If Elaine had been going to kill herself, she'd have written a book about it first. And I don't think she'd kill herself, anyway."

"Yeah. I'm betting she didn't swallow the pills. She got fed them."

"People are going to tell you she was depressed, though," I said.

"Yeah."

"You know about this?"

"Not much."

"She lost a patient," I said. "She was a therapist. You already know that, right? A psychologist. She knew Rita." Since Kevin lives next door, and Rita has my second-floor apartment, he knows Rita, too, of course. "Anyway, that's why Elaine had the dog, because of her patient."

"Could you stop talking about dogs?"

"They're relevant," I said. "She had a patient who killed herself, and she left the dog to Elaine. Elaine never even had a dog before, and she took Kimi mostly because of that. Because she felt terrible about having one of her patients commit suicide. So she took the dog partly out of guilt. I mean, this was the only thing she could do for her, she said. But, of course, Kimi is a beautiful bitch. Any sane person would want her. I'm sure the minute Elaine saw her, she knew she had to have her."

"People," Kevin said. "No more dogs."

"So the point is that Elaine really was upset, and people are going to tell you she was depressed, and, okay, maybe she was. That's probably one of the reasons she let the dog push her around. That's what I was helping with. She hadn't exactly made herself the alpha figure in Kimi's life."

"Alpha. It's Greek to me!" Kevin sounded gleeful. Then he repeated himself in case I'd been too slow to catch on the first time.

I hissed. I'm not a total misfit in Cambridge, and that's what you're supposed to do here when someone makes a pun. "Anyway," I said, "Kimi was top dog. Alpha is what it's called in wolf packs. Elaine was a definite beta—underdog—with Kimi. So maybe one thing that happened was that with this patient, Elaine was top dog. I mean, she was the therapist. She'd have to be, wouldn't she? So maybe with Kimi, she was afraid of that power. Look what happened last time."

Rita would have loved that, but Kevin wasn't interested. He was interested in the patient.

"So who was this patient?" he asked.

"I don't know. Some woman. Elaine said she was young."

"And how did she die?"

"Suicide. An overdose, Elaine said. That's all I know. I remember, because I thought about cocaine, because of, you know, how the Celtics are doing. Anyway, it wasn't an accident. She left a note for Elaine. She asked Elaine to take her dog."

"No more dog talk."

"Let me tell you something," I said. "You think I don't care about Elaine, right? That's the implication. Well, I do. I'm telling you about the dog because the dog is relevant. I feel terrible about Elaine. You know, in a way, you could say she was my patient, because she needed help with Kimi, and not psychotherapy, either. And I was helping. I did care about her. We were getting to be friends."

"She didn't tell you the name of the patient?"

"No. I suppose she thought it was confidential. Therapists don't tell you who their patients are. It's some kind of ethical violation. I don't know who she was."

"Me neither," Kevin said. "But I will."

Bailing Kimi out was easy. I didn't need Kevin's intervention on our behalf. Malamutes don't ruff-ruff and bow-wow like other dogs. They talk. That's what it's called. "Woo-woo," they say. "Ah woo. Woooooo?" Kimi had been doing more than talking. She'd been shouting, swearing, and trying to start cage fights with the dogs in the other pens. She was very dominant, and as soon as she'd found herself in a pack of strange dogs, she'd simply tried to establish her position. I started to explain her behavior, but no one wanted to hear about it. Everyone at the pound was as glad to get rid of her as I was to get her.

Chapter 4

KEVIN Dennehy's mother sees faces as a series of animated maps inscribing themselves on the human countenance. Kevin, she always says, has the map of Ireland written on his face. Rita has Italy. I have Scotland.

"Hey, Holly, how ya doing?"

Kevin was standing at my back door. In one beefy arm, he held a brown paper grocery bag. Although he doesn't like to hear his living situation phrased this way, he lives with his mother in her vegetarian, teetotal house—Mrs. Dennehy has abandoned the Catholic Church for Seventh-Day Adventism—and, whether he admits it or not, it's definitely her house. Before I bought the house next door to hers, or should I say, before my father helped me with the down payment (when I couldn't find a decent apartment that allowed pets), Kevin lived mostly on pecan loaf and herbal tea except when he went out for pepperoni pizza, McDonald's quarter-pounders, and Kentucky Fried Chicken. If Kevin wanted a Bud, he'd have to sneak one on the back steps, and if Mrs. Dennehy caught him, he'd have to sit on the curb or pace up and down the sidewalk to drink it. He didn't like the image of a cop drinking in public, but the solution he found—slipping the beer can into a paper bag—didn't exactly raise the tone of the neighborhood, and people complained.

In spite of the block-long town-house complex that Harvard has just erected across the street on Concord Avenue, the corner of Appleton and Concord isn't the toniest place in Cambridge. The upwardly mobile triple-deckers can't help giving away their working-class origins. Some, like Mrs. Dennehy's, remain aggressively proletarian and proud of it, too, with plebe-

ian lime-green vinyl and mock-brick siding, pitted aluminum
storm doors, and scraggly barberry hedges mocking the pretensions of the newly genteel pale-painted façades, railroad-tie fir
bark, and spreading dwarf junipers of their neighbors.

So it isn't the toniest neighborhood—it'll never be Brattle
Street—but getting Kevin and his bagged beer cans off the sidewalk and into my kitchen helped almost as much as the town
houses. Kevin keeps his Bud in my refrigerator, and I let him
cook meat, not that what he does deserves to be called cooking.
My own cooking consists mainly of scrambling eggs, slapping
sandwiches together, spooning out cottage cheese, baking dog
biscuits and liver treats, dishing up dog food, and refilling water
bowls, but at least I don't burn everything the way Kevin does.

"How am I doing, Kevin? I am holding up." My voice probably sounded a little hoarse, not from shouting at Rowdy and
Kimi, of course, but from speaking sweet reason to both of
them. "It takes three days, you know," I added. "Anyone who
knows anything about dogs will tell you that. Introduce a second dog into an only-dog house, and it takes a minimum of
three days. I'm sorry about the noise last night. Did it wake
you up?"

"My mother woke me up." He dumped the bag on the
counter and pulled out a package of hamburger. Rowdy ran
to the counter, pricked up his hears, raised his big head, sniffed
hopefully, and tried to look cute. "She had this bad dream,"
Kevin added. "A nightmare. About a beast with seven heads.
All of the heads were yelping like dogs."

"What a coincidence. I had the same nightmare. An apoca-
lyptic vision visited the neighborhood." Then I noticed that his
face was, for once, showing fatigue. "Look, seriously, I'm
sorry. This won't go on forever."

Rowdy had been sleeping in my room off and on since the
first night I brought him home. The floor under the bay window, where the window seat is going to go when I have the
money, belonged to him. I couldn't ask him to give it up or
push over. But what really did it was the old Nylabone of
Rowdy's that Kimi discovered under the bedroom radiator at
three A.M. and refused to relinquish.

"So where is she?" Kevin asked.

"In the yard. Digging, probably." For January in Cambridge, it was a warm day, in the forties, and Rowdy and I had

both felt desperate for some relief. The previous summer, I'd finally persuaded Rowdy to abandon work on the scale model of the battlefield at Verdun on which he'd been laboring, but Kimi was probably excavating all the trenches and foxholes I'd filled in. At least she wasn't bothering the neighbors. She was quiet, and the yard is fenced.

"Sinequan," Kevin said.

"What?"

"Sinequan. Not a trace of cocaine anywhere. Sinequan. Also called doxepin." The skillet was smoking. Kevin dropped in two hamburger patties that sizzled, spattered, and emitted bursts of greasy steam.

"What is it?" I asked. "Sleeping pills?"

"Sometimes. They say it's for people who are depressed and nervous at the same time. Antidepressant and tranquilizer. Sleepiness is a side effect, and sometimes people take it for that."

"Well, I guess you could say Elaine was depressed and nervous, sort of. I mean, she was depressed and upset about her patient. But I don't know. She didn't strike me as someone who'd take pills for it. Like Rita, you know?"

"Yeah." He turned the hamburgers burned-side up.

"With Rita, everything's an issue she's supposed to work on, confront. Right? If she gets a headache, she practically won't take aspirin because she thinks the headache means something. And if she takes aspirin, she thinks she's just running away from whatever the psychological issue is, and she feels guilty. I mean, if everybody gets the flu, and Rita does, too, she still thinks it isn't just the flu. It's her body sending her a message about her mother. Or if she admits it's the flu, she has to analyze why she got it. I would've thought Elaine was like that, too. Did she have a prescription for this stuff? Was there a bottle there?"

"Nope."

"That doesn't necessarily mean much, especially if she was using it to sleep. People hand stuff around."

That's Cambridge. You say you haven't been sleeping too well, and ten people offer you their Xanax or Ativan before they even hear that what you've got is a noisy dog, not insomnia. And when you tell them, they say to take some yourself and give the rest to the dog.

"Do people tell you to mix the stuff with cottage cheese first?"

I looked at him.

"Cottage cheese." He turned the hamburgers again. "That's how she took it. They're both in her, Sinequan and cottage cheese, mixed with a lot of other stuff, and the carton shows traces. Like I been saying, she got fed it. Now we know in what. In cottage cheese."

"God. It's lucky Kimi didn't get any."

"The carton hadn't been licked clean." Kevin deposited the two blackened lumps on the bottoms of two cold hamburger rolls, put them on separate plates, topped each lump with a big spoonful of mayonnaise and a dollop of ketchup, balanced the tops of the rolls on the lumps, and pushed down hard. He slid one plate onto the kitchen table in front of me and sat down with the other in front of him.

"But," I said, "she could've fed some to Kimi. I always used to do that, give cottage cheese to my dogs. A lot of breeders used to recommend it. Then I guess it went out of style. Anyway, Elaine probably wouldn't have thought about supplementing Kimi's food. She didn't know anything about dogs. And, obviously, Kimi's fine. She was okay when you found her, wasn't she?"

"Yeah. Ran up and tried to make friends, like Rowdy does." The ketchup and mayonnaise dripped from his hands and down his wrists like the seepage from an infected wound. "Don't you want that?" He pointed to the plate in front of me.

"I just ate, Kevin, but thanks. You have it."

"Anyhow, the dog was fine. She growled just like Rowdy does, and I got one of the guys to take her out. She'd chewed up some stuff in the living room. A pillow. Some kind of big basket."

Navajo, Elaine had said when I'd asked where it came from. It was a big red and black basket, about three feet across, woven with a pattern of what looked like eagles. I could have helped Elaine to stop Kimi from ruining things like that. I started to imagine how we'd do it. But, of course, we wouldn't. Elaine and Kimi didn't have that great future together anymore.

"So how did it happen?" I asked. "Somebody mixed this stuff with her cottage cheese, and she ate it and died. That's it?"

"Yeah. After she ate it, which was at night, supper, she must have just felt tired. She went to bed. And then everything just slowed way, way down, and she stopped breathing."

Elaine was not the kind of person who would have wanted to go gentle into that good night. It seemed doubly unfair that she hadn't had a chance to fight back.

"The question," Kevin said, "is how and when it got into the cottage cheese. It could've been after it was in her refrigerator. Or before."

"Did it come from the milkman? You must've seen the box by the door. Pleasant Valley. They deliver cottage cheese. I order it sometimes." It's one of those perfect foods: You can feed it to your dogs or eat it yourself. "It's good cottage cheese. It's better than the kind you buy in stores, and it's fresher, I think."

"You got some now?"

"Plain or chive?" Kevin has a big appetite—in spite of his bulk, he's a runner—but it still seemed odd.

"Just the carton."

The one I gave him was an ordinary white plastic sixteen-ounce carton showing the dairy's name and the same cow logo that's on the milk boxes. Kevin wiped his hands on a paper towel, removed the lid, and examined the container and its contents.

"You've opened this already?" he asked.

"No. Look, it's full. It hasn't been touched."

"But you opened it."

"No. I haven't touched it."

"So where's the, uh, the plastic thing? The plastic strip. You know, to unseal it."

"Those tamper-proof things? The ones from the milkman don't have those. I mean, they aren't going to sit around in stores or anything. They aren't all sealed up. You just take the lid off. It's just like the old days."

He replaced the lid on the carton, removed it again, looked hard at the cottage cheese, and replaced the lid.

"So it's the same kind?" I asked.

He nodded.

"Well," I said, "you can't buy it in stores. They don't carry this kind. You can't get it anywhere except from the milkman."

"So it would've sat out in the milk box. It would've sat there until she brought it in."

"Yes."

We looked at each other.

"And," I added, "anybody could've come along, opened the milk box, opened the carton, added anything, and closed the carton again. If the cottage cheese was smoothed out, nobody could've told the difference. And Elaine's milk box is on the porch, and it's screened from the street. You know?"

"Yeah. Actually, I do know."

"So," I said, "it wasn't necessarily somebody who got inside her house. It could have been anybody."

"Yeah," Kevin said. "That eliminates a lot of people."

"Maybe it was some antifeminist, like the guy in Montreal. It could've been somebody who didn't even know her, some guy who hated her because his wife read her books and left him. Or maybe some woman took one of her assertiveness workshops, told some guy to go to hell, and he blamed Elaine. Something like that. Anybody who knew where she lived."

"And found out she had a milkman," Kevin said.

"It's not so unusual. The yuppies do it because it's convenient, and so do families with a lot of kids. And some people just like the idea of having a milkman. Also, the glass bottles are ecological, right? There must be at least two dairies that deliver around here."

"If somebody knew she got cottage cheese. . . . "

"Yeah," I said. "So either it was somebody who'd been in her house and seen it there, in the refrigerator, and asked her about it or something. Or he just knew that you get that kind from Pleasant Valley and no place else. Or somebody looked in the milk box after the milkman had been there and before Elaine took it inside. You know, Kevin, that could have been a long time. Those boxes are insulated. You can leave milk and things in them for hours, all day. Suppose the milkman came in the morning. If Elaine was at work all day, the cottage cheese probably sat there until she came home. So you need to talk to the milkman."

"No kidding."

"He's a nice guy," I said. "At least, if it's the same one I have. It probably is. It must be the same route. He's a very nice guy. He's going to be awfully upset. So is the dairy, if this ends up in the papers. And anybody could've found out where she lived. She was listed in the phone book. I know because I looked her number up the other day."

"Anybody," he said. "Anybody who wanted her dead. But the thing is, this patient of hers. I tracked that down."

"And?"

"She did die of an overdose. Funny how these things happen. Her name was Donna Zalewski. She took an overdose of Sinequan."

"Just like Elaine."

"Just like Elaine."

Chapter 5

"THERE'S one hitch," Rita said. "It so happens that Elaine hated cottage cheese."

"How do you know?" I asked.

We were in Rita's living room, which is directly above mine and the same shape, also with a fireplace. In most other respects, though, the two rooms look like the before and after pictures in the interior-decorating magazines. My living room is the before. A cheap glass globe covers the original overhead bulb. There is one couch. Rita has color-coordinated furniture from stores like Bloomingdale's. Come to think of it, although Rita and I don't look alike, she's the after of herself, and I'm permanently before.

"I knew her," Rita said. "Remember? We were in that supervision group together." She was wearing her one pair of jeans and a white vicuna sweater. To sit around the apartment, she'd put on a pair of big handcrafted gold earrings and a matching chain.

"Did you spend a lot of time discussing dairy products?" I asked.

"We had occasion to refer to the milkman."

"That must have been fascinating."

"It was," Rita said. "Elaine had a dream about him. He represented male nurturance. Milk?"

Rita says things like that sometimes, but she's very good to her dog, a white-muzzled, untrained dachshund named Groucho, who was sitting in her lap.

"You must be kidding."

"I'm serious. We did a lot with dreams in the group."

"So she had a premonition?"

"Of course not. It's just peculiar. She was one of those people with an aversion to yogurt, things like that. Sour cream, cottage cheese."

"So why'd she have a milkman?"

"For milk, presumably," Rita said. "On the surface of things at least. But, obviously, the milkman had symbolic significance for her."

"Actually, she did drink milk. At least in tea, she did. I know because I like milk in my tea, and when she put the milk out, Kimi drank it. And I'm sure I remember Elaine using it in her tea . . . Would somebody like that cook with it? With cottage cheese?"

"Why not? She wasn't *phobic* about it. And if you make a casserole or a dip or something, you don't really taste it, do you? And the texture is different."

"Yeah, but even so, she ate something she didn't like," I said. "That's what's really strange. What a weird thing for someone to put the stuff in. I mean, if you wanted to kill her, wouldn't that be the last thing you'd put it in?"

"You'd want something she always ate," Rita said.

"Suppose you're going to murder Mrs. Dennehy," I said. "What would you put something in? Pecans. Herbal tea. Right? You'd sprinkle arsenic or whatever on something she eats all the time."

"But only if you knew," Rita said. "If this guy was after her because she was a feminist, how would he know? Maybe he just watched her house, noticed the milkman, and decided to lace whatever was in the milk box."

"So why did he use the same thing her patient used? Sinequan."

"Maybe there's a connection," Rita said. I didn't pay too much attention. Therapists are always saying that everything is connected to everything else. "Maybe it was meant to look as if she were repeating the suicide. Her patient takes a fatal overdose of Sinequan. Elaine loses the patient. She identifies with her. To keep the patient alive, defend against her guilt, she becomes her lost patient. But it doesn't really work. Or it works too well. And she does just what the patient did."

"But that's not what happened."

"No. But maybe that's the picture somebody tried to create."

"It's awfully psychological," I said. "The police probably wouldn't buy it."

"So who was this patient? What do you know about her?"

"Practically nothing. Except that she owned Kimi, of course. Elaine said she was very troubled, or something like that. Her name was Donna Zalewski. Kevin told me that. Elaine didn't."

Rita's face lost its expression. "No," she said. "Elaine wouldn't have told you that. It would have been a breach of ethics."

The temperature outside was back down to normal, about ten degrees, and I was listening for the milkman and still trying to write about the woman who died and came to life as her own dog. Rowdy and Kimi heard the milkman before I did. Their relationship was improving slightly (Kimi occasionally remembered that she was inhabiting territory that Rowdy had claimed first and that he outweighed her by fifteen pounds), but they were still highly competitive, and one of their favorite competitions was a race to see who could get to the door first. Kimi weighed about seventy-five pounds, and Rowdy was up to ninety. My father, who raises wolf dog hybrids, had always wanted Rowdy to look even more like a wolf than he did already. Buck kept telling me to keep Rowdy down to eighty-five, but Faith Barlow, who was handling him in breed, had insisted that I was starving him. Buck and Faith both kept delivering lectures on dog food, too. Buck maintained that Eukanuba was the wrong food for a malamute who wasn't worked in harness every day, and Faith insisted that it was the perfect food. Peace never reigns in dogdom.

Anyway, at the sound of heavy steps and the clatter of milk bottles, a hundred and sixty-five pounds of Alaskan malamute muscled its way to the back door, where Rowdy, who'd finally got his C.D.—his first obedience title, Companion Dog—sat the way I'd taught him, and Kimi raised her big right front paw and gouged another line of claw marks through the terracotta paint and into the wood. Rowdy's big white face bore a look of condescending superiority, civilization sneering at barbarity. He tilted his big head down toward her and raised it up to me.

"Good boy, Rowdy," I said. "Kimi, no. Cut that out."

I shut them both in the kitchen and opened the back door.

Jim, the milkman, was a nice guy who had told me he lived in Dorchester with a wife, four kids, and a mixed-breed dog that was supposed to be half Labrador retriever.

"Don't bother," I said to him as he started to put my order in the milk box. "I'll take it in."

"Sure thing," he said. "Cold enough for you?"

"Cold enough for my dogs," I said. "I've got a new one. Another malamute."

"Good for you."

"She used to belong to one of your customers, I heard. You do Upland Road?"

"You bet."

"Elaine Walsh."

His face clouded over. "The lady who died."

"Yeah. You know about . . ."

"You still want this cottage cheese?"

"Yes."

"It ain't in the papers," he said. "But I guess you heard already."

"You worried about people canceling?"

He just sighed.

"I hope that doesn't happen," I said. "If it does, I don't think it'll last long."

We talked a little about how worried he was about losing business. Then, since it was a little chilly to be out in jeans and a sweatshirt, I got to the point. "Tell me something. Did Elaine Walsh always get cottage cheese? Was it part of her regular order?"

"Yeah. Like I told them," Jim said, meaning the police, I assumed, "just lately. Before, milk, eggs, butter. Then she changed the regular order, added the cottage cheese. Plain. A pound. Twice a week."

It took me two trips to take my own order in, first the milk, then the eggs and the cottage cheese. I put the carton of cottage cheese on the counter and began transferring the eggs to the plastic container in the refrigerator door, but before I finished, I had to stop and grab Kimi. She'd been bouncing around and wagging her tail, but now she rose up, rested both front paws on the counter, and started sniffing the cottage cheese carton.

All canine behavior is communication, of course. The dog may not intend to tell you anything, but if you observe care-

fully, you see that everything a dog does tells you something.
Kimi's behavior was easy to read. She recognized that carton. *Dinnertime,* she was saying. *My dinner. My food. This is
mine.* Elaine hadn't liked cottage cheese. She hadn't bought it
until recently; in other words, until she'd acquired a dog. Kimi
was telling me that Elaine bought that cottage cheese for her.
Just as in my story, Elaine had come back to life as her own
dog.

"Kevin? Holly. Look, Elaine wasn't murdered, exactly."
Again, I'd had to call him at the station. "She died by accident.
I know you have this irrational idea that I'm obsessed with
dogs, but listen. The cottage cheese was meant for Kimi. Elaine
didn't order cottage cheese from the milkman until she got
Kimi."

"I know," Kevin said.

"Elaine hated cottage cheese. And when Kimi sees the carton, she knows it's for her. It wasn't meant for Elaine at all.
It was meant for Kimi. Her first owner died from an overdose
of Sinequan, and her second owner died the same way. And
I'm her third owner . . ."

"Don't eat anything," Kevin said. "Don't eat anything
you've already bought. Are you busy for dinner?"

"No."

Steve had a clinic from four until eight.

"We'll go out. Don't eat anything until I get there."

Tell that to an Alaskan malamute. Jim had actually handed
me the cottage cheese, and I was positive it was okay. Almost.
I would have been positive, of course, if he hadn't been Elaine's
milkman. Jim? Impossible. I put the cottage cheese down the
garbage disposal, rinsed out the carton, threw it in the trash,
and carried the trash outside to the barrels where Kimi couldn't
steal the carton. And dog food? In the kitchen closet sat what
was left of a forty-pound bag of Eukanuba, premium dog chow
with a guaranteed minimum protein content of thirty percent.
In the United States, about four hundred major manufacturers
and hundreds of little companies produce God knows how
many thousand brands and varieties of dog food. In spite of
Faith Barlow's brand loyalty, I won't swear that Eukanuba is
any better than ANF or a couple of the other premium foods,
but it's much better than hundreds and hundreds of other

brands, and Faith trusts it, especially for a good coat. I'd paid mightily for it, and I wouldn't have thrown out twenty pounds on a whim. Who'd been in my kitchen since I'd brought Kimi home? Had anyone I didn't know been alone there? The man who'd repaired the oven. Someone else? I couldn't remember. With Rowdy and Kimi growling at each other, I sealed the open bag in a heavy-duty plastic garbage bag, carried it outside, and put it in a trash barrel with a lid that locks on. I checked the lid to make sure it was tight. Not everyone obeys the leash law, and (although I knew, really knew, that the dog food was fine) I didn't want to risk killing someone else's dog while saving my own.

Then I put a training collar and a leash on each of the dogs and walked them to the Sage's at the corner of Concord and Huron, where I bought a small bag of Purina. On the way home, they had a near fight, snarls and scuffle but no blood, over an apple core someone had discarded on the icy sidewalk, but I managed to yank both of them away from it. I knew there was nothing wrong with it, of course. I knew that no one had put anything in it and left it for my dogs. Or for Kimi in particular. I knew that. I didn't let them have it, anyway.

Chapter 6

"LET'S get one thing straight," Kevin said. "This is all supposition on your part."

My favorite restaurant in Cambridge used to be a now-defunct place in Kendall Square called the Daily Catch—squid, shrimp, and mussels with garlic and olive oil—but the only time Kevin went there he saw someone else eating black pasta (squid ink, I suppose), and he decided that the Daily Catch was a yuppie hangout and refused to return. He'd insisted on an upscale pizzeria, and we were paying about sixteen dollars a pizza for some okay crust with hardly any sauce.

"I understand," I said. "I'm not stupid. There are two possibilities. One, the guy didn't know Elaine or didn't know her well. He assumed she ate what she bought. He didn't know she hated cottage cheese."

"Good pizza," Kevin said.

"Bland," I said. "The crust isn't too bad. Anyway, he didn't know that the cottage cheese was for Kimi, and he meant the Sinequan for Elaine, not Kimi. Second possibility, he knew Elaine, knew she hated cottage cheese, assumed she fed it all to her dog, and meant to kill Kimi. You talked to Jim, right? The milkman?"

"Yeah. Says he didn't know about the dog."

"He knew she had one," I said. "Anyone would. Elaine quit trying to walk Kimi because Kimi pulled so hard she'd knock Elaine over, and Elaine thought she was going for other dogs. So Elaine just took her out to the flower bed in front of the house, and once in a while, about half a block down the street. Take one look. You can see that a dog's been there."

"The guy's not all that swift."

"How swift would he need to be? She's a big bitch. The evidence isn't exactly subtle. You could be really slow and still figure a cat hadn't left all that. And could we talk about something else? This isn't exactly dinner-table conversation."

"So maybe he knew she had a dog," Kevin said. "Maybe he figured it was a neighbor's. Says he didn't know the cottage cheese was for a dog, didn't know Elaine Walsh. He'd see her now and then. She'd pay him or ask for something extra. That's all. She wasn't friendly, he says."

"She had a dream about him," I said. "Rita told me. Anyhow, the point is that if the Sinequan was meant for Elaine, the murderer was someone who didn't know her, or didn't know her very well. And if it was meant for Kimi, the murderer was somebody who did know Elaine, somebody who knew her well enough to know she didn't like cottage cheese, that she bought it for her dog. This is stingy pizza. It's practically all crust."

"You've eaten your half," Kevin said.

"So what was in her stomach?"

"Sinequan. Cottage cheese. Noodles. Tomato sauce. Meat of some kind, sausages. Red wine."

"Lasagna," I said. "I get it. She used it instead of ricotta."

"I'd never have guessed," Kevin said. "Unless she happened to leave the cookbook out in one of those clear plastic stands."

"Oh. And I suppose she did?"

"Yes."

"Was it lasagna?"

"No. Some mixture with noodles."

"That makes more sense. People who live alone don't usually make something like lasagna. A pan of it feeds ten people. If you make it for yourself, you have to eat it for weeks. Do you want that last slice?"

"You need it more than I do," he said. "Besides, the anchovies were your idea."

"So which is it? Which one was he after? Elaine or Kimi?"

"It's more complicated than that. Because of this Donna Zalewski. Elaine Walsh's patient. But it seems like she had a prescription."

"Not from Elaine she didn't. Elaine was a psychologist, like Rita. She wasn't an M.D. She couldn't prescribe."

"From a guy Elaine Walsh sent her to. Some psychiatrist. Benjamin Moss, his name is."

"Never heard of him," I said. "I wonder if Rita knows him. Hey, you know what? Rita has this theory. She thinks maybe somebody set this up to look as if Elaine had sort of mimicked her patient's suicide. Anyway, she doesn't think that's what Elaine did. Just that somebody tried to make it look like that. Does that make any sense?"

Kevin shrugged and made a face.

"But," I added, "she just swallowed the pills, didn't she? The patient. I mean . . ."

"So it seemed at the time," Kevin said.

"Were you there? You were involved in it?"

"Me personally?"

"Yes."

"No."

"Okay, so you don't want to say it, right? You didn't see everything for yourself, and you don't want to take somebody's word for what there was to see. So there's a lot you don't know. Anyhow, am I being crazy? Maybe the Sinequan was meant for Elaine, but not because she was Elaine. Because she owned Kimi. That's possible, isn't it?"

"Possible."

"So somebody could've been after whoever owns Kimi. Okay. But why?"

"It's not the only possibility. It's just one."

"Yeah. Only this time, I happen to be the one. Or the guy screwed up both times. Both times he was after Kimi, and he got her owners instead."

"Unlikely. Donna Zalewski left a note."

"Okay."

"But just to be on the safe side," Kevin said, "don't eat any dog food for a while." He was beaming. Then his big face turned serious, and he rested one of his hefty fists on the table. "Look, I don't know what the hell is going on. That's the truth. Until I do, watch what you eat. Watch what you feed those dogs."

"I always watch what I feed my dogs. What kind of person do you think I am?"

*   *   *

If you want a really ferocious dog fight, you need two of the same sex, especially two bitches, but nevertheless, Kimi and Rowdy got into a championship bout the next morning, and it was all my fault. Having thrown out all their food, I needed to drive to a pet supply place—needless to say, Eukanuba isn't supermarket dog chow—and decided to take them along (good idea) loose in the back of my Bronco (bad idea). My first mistake was not having cleaned the Bronco since my last trip to Maine. My second was putting Kimi in first. My third was putting Rowdy in at all.

Kimi hopped in and discovered a half-eaten blueberry muffin tucked under the front passenger seat, and when Rowdy bounded in after her, he went for the muffin. And her. Miss Alpha Wolf, of course, refused to part with her prey, and Rowdy leapt on her, dug his teeth into the back of her neck, and pinned her. With Kimi yelping in pain and Rowdy snarling and biting, I had no choice, and luckily, I was wearing heavy Thinsulate gloves (L. L. Bean, of course). I jumped into the back of the Bronco, straddled Rowdy, and grabbed his collar with my left hand. Rowdy'd pinned Kimi, and in pinning him, I found myself riding two writhing, bucking malamutes. I hung on and used my right hand to force Rowdy's jaw open. As you may know, the trick is to wrap your hand over the top of the muzzle and push in hard at the hinges of the upper and lower jaws, way back where there aren't any molars. I won't try it with any dog except my own, and I keep talking to remind the dog of who I am. As soon as Rowdy'd released his hold on Kimi, who wasn't yet my dog the way Rowdy was, she slashed out and got my parka and a glove, but no flesh. Then she spotted a bit of muffin that she'd dropped in the scuffle, and while she darted for it and tossed it down her throat, I pulled Rowdy out of the Bronco and slammed the tailgate.

If I'd left them both home, they'd have won, and I'd have lost the leadership of our little pack. They accompanied me, each in a large, solid polypropylene dog crate, the kind you see at airports.

"Freedom presupposes an educated populace," I explained to them.

As I drove to one of the western suburbs to pick up the dog food, the adrenaline was still running, and I was feeling confident, mostly because of what I'd told Elaine about dogs, power, and self-confidence. Alaskan malamutes aren't the biggest dogs in the world, but when you take size into account, they're probably the strongest, and Rowdy and Kimi combined outweighed me by fifty pounds. Once you've broken up a fight between those two growling hulks of flashing teeth and Arctic muscle, what mere person can intimidate you?

A sneaky one. A coward. The kind who won't confront you directly. The kind who makes you afraid to eat and afraid to feed your dogs.

Well, not me, I thought. If you're after Kimi or after her owner, you picked the wrong dog and the wrong owner. I can tackle two Alaskan malamutes and come out on top. You don't scare me.

On the drive home, I planned it out.

"First we find out about you, Kimi," I said to her. "We find out who you are, where you came from, and I'll bet it isn't far away because they don't breed malamutes like you outside New England. They've never even seen a malamute like you." As I've said, big as any malamute is by ordinary standards, mine were comparatively small. In other parts of the country, and occasionally here, too, you see M'Loot malamutes that stand more than twenty-eight inches at the withers. (That's where you measure a dog's height, at the highest part of his body, between the neck and shoulders.) In other ways, too, Kimi and Rowdy both looked like Kotzebues, the original malamutes bred in New England, where we know that bigger isn't necessarily better.

"And," I added, "if there's nothing strange about who you are, we check out the remote possibility that in spite of your faultless behavior, you've done something to offend someone. And we find out what happened to your other owners, right, girl? Because if you lose your third in a row, you and Rowdy will both end up with a charming gentleman in Owls Head, Maine, who'll breed you both to wolves. And in the meantime, we're careful. We don't take candy from strangers."

Chapter 7

"WHAT you are is a fool," Faith Barlow said to me. When she smiles, her eyes twinkle and dimples appear, but she wasn't smiling. "Wasting your time in obedience. With malamutes."

Faith had nothing against malamutes. In fact, she was rubbing the fur around Kimi's neck, and Buddy, her oldest malamute, was lying on the carpet of her living room. At the moment, Faith had eleven other malamutes and was planning a litter for the spring.

"And furthermore, she added, "you could have reserved one. It's going to be a nice litter. Bounce and Dasher. It's a repeat breeding. Why didn't you let me know you wanted one?" She'd looked just the same for as long as I'd known her, her light brown hair streaked with gray, her face apparently fixed at forty. She'd been breeding and handling malamutes for years. Spending all that time with pushy dogs had taught her to be direct. "It wasn't the money, was it?"

"No. Kimi was the one I wanted," I said. "I don't know what you're bitching about. She's one of yours, after all. It isn't as if I'd gone off and got a puppy from somewhere else."

The couch and chairs in Faith's living room aren't shaped like dogs and aren't fur-covered, and the lamps are not brass malamutes packing light bulbs and lampshades on their backs. Faith is capable of occasional restraint. Over the fireplace, however, hangs an oil painting of her foundation bitch, Beebee. There are more than enough miniature ceramic malamutes lined up on the mantelpiece to form two or three teams. One wall is filled with shelves that hold silver-plated trophies, pewter plates, and glass statuary interspersed with china sled dogs. The wall space that isn't covered with photographs of mala-

39

mutes displays framed pedigrees and awards. On a side table
sit three dinner-size plates with hand-painted portraits of three
of Faith's dogs. It's amazing that Faith has that couch and
those chairs. You'd expect to be offered a seat on a dog sled.

"And as for obedience," I continued, "Rowdy has his C.D.,
and we're training for Open. We're going to enter the matches
in the early spring and do the trials in the summer."

Have I mentioned Rowdy's C.D.? A Companion Dog title
is nothing special for a golden retriever or one of the other
breeds you see all the time in obedience, just a grammar school
diploma, but for a malamute, especially Rowdy, it's pretty
good. Open is what you enter when you're going for the next
title, C.D.X., Companion Dog Excellent. In the United States,
about one malamute a year gets a C.D.X., which is one reason
Faith thought I was wasting my time. But I wanted Rowdy
to be that one.

"Good luck," Faith said. "And I'm not trying to drum up
business, you know. I don't need it. I could sell more puppies
than I could breed just this year. If I bred all three bitches, I
could sell all the puppies. To show homes, too."

A show home is every breeder's ideal, owners who'll show
the puppy in breed, not just keep him as a pet, but a good, con-
scientious breeder also cares about finding responsible, loving
owners who'll give the dog a happy life.

"So how did you end up selling Kimi to Donna Zalewski?"
I asked. "Did she promise to show her?"

"No. Look, I felt sorry for her. She needed a dog. She was
crazy about dogs, and she told me this whole long story about
a malamute some neighbors had when she was a kid. And I
knew she had the resources." What Faith meant is that there
are people who'll pay five hundred or a thousand dollars for
a dog when they don't have the spare cash to feed the dog or
pay one vet bill. The same people make big down payments on
Corvettes and Jaguars when they can't afford to refill the gas
tanks. "You can't always tell what people are like. I try to
screen people, but sometimes I'm wrong."

"Did you have a return agreement?"

Faith looked insulted. "Of course. You know I won't sell a
puppy without one." A return agreement means that the
breeder will take the dog back. If the dog develops hip dysplasia

or bites someone, the buyer returns him. Try that with a pet shop. "I don't know why she left Kimi to that woman."

"Elaine was her therapist," I said.

"Even so! It's not as if Donna hadn't stayed in touch with me. I'd talked to her maybe two months before. She knew I'd have taken Kimi back if I'd known she was that desperate."

"It didn't have to do with you, Faith. Apparently, it had something to do with her relationship with her therapist. Like leaving part of herself to Elaine? Something like that."

"That's bull." Faith said. "This woman had never even had a dog before."

"You got it."

"And nobody even called me." Perhaps in response to Faith's hurt tone, Kimi sprang halfway into her lap and licked her face, but Faith, used to tricks like that, shoved Kimi off.

"These aren't people who would have thought to call you," I said. "Elaine Walsh had the registration papers, and she'd done the transfer of ownership, but that was only because Donna's lawyer found Kimi's papers and told Elaine what to do. He has poodles himself. He shows. Otherwise, Elaine wouldn't have thought of the papers. She wouldn't have known they existed."

Kimi's American Kennel Club registration papers were how I'd traced her to Faith Barlow. I'd had to show Kevin Dennehy a couple of AKC registration forms and beg him to see if there was something similar in Elaine's house. There had been, and he'd brought me a photocopy. The breeder's name was on the papers, of course. And Kimi's official name, too. It was worse than my own. Sno-Kist Qimissung. My bitch. I'd have to live with it.

"So how do you plan on getting ownership transferred to you?" Faith asked.

"I haven't worked out the details," I said, "but I'm not worried. It'll work out. The executor of Elaine's estate will be able to sign, I guess. It won't be a problem. It'll just take a while. What does her name mean, anyway?"

"Snowdrift," Faith said. "It's Inuit. Eskimo."

The most frequent letters in the Inuit language seem to be *q, g,* and *l,* and trying to say the words gives me a sore throat, but Inuits probably find English equally tough. Dog names like Lady and Blackie are probably so unpronounceable in Inuit that Lady and Blackie eventually end up with euphonious Inuit call names like Qllgg and Lgqqlq.

Faith went on. "Donna found it in a book. You see? There's a good example of why I thought she was okay. The minute I met her, I knew there was something spacey about her, flaky, but you could tell she cared about dogs, and she read up on malamutes, the whole thing. Even before she picked up the puppy. That always impresses me, when a new owner reads up on the breed. And then when she came for the puppy, she had a new crate in the car, everything all set up. And naturally, I gave her a whole schedule of when she'd need shots, what to feed her, when: everything. And the same day, I remember, she called me to ask about something. Vitamin supplements."

"Did you tell her to feed cottage cheese?"

"Yeah. I always do. Why?"

"I just wondered."

"Why?"

"Relax. She probably did everything you told her. What was she like, anyway?"

"Pretty. Striking, really. Tall, with her hair messy, in a fashionable way, like on TV. You know? Ten years ago, it would've looked like a bad home permanent or like she hadn't combed it in a week, but now it's the style. But I didn't figure her for one of those—the ones who just want a flashy dog to be seen with. First time she was here, I let two of them loose out in the yard, and Mickey jumped all over her, got mud on her clothes, and it didn't faze her at all. She just said he reminded her of this malamute she'd grown up with."

"I guess if she hadn't seemed okay . . ."

"What do you want me to do? Send every prospective owner to a shrink? I do my best. Yeah, she seemed a little nervous. She'd kind of look off into the blue. But you can't refuse to sell to every person who acts a little odd."

Faith senses something untrustworthy in the character of any person who owns fewer than six dogs and doesn't spend every weekend commuting five or six hundred miles to dog shows.

"No, you can't," I said.

"And she did call me once in hysterics, but, hey, it happens, right?"

"What was it about?"

"Nothing. The puppy vomited. I don't know why she called me and not a vet. People do it. Anyway, it was nothing. I called her back a few days later, and she'd practically forgotten she'd called me."

"You got a funny look on your face when I mentioned Donna Zalewski," I said to Rita. "The same funny look you've got now."

"Oh." She locked her teeth together and clamped her jaw shut.

We were walking Rowdy and Groucho down Concord Avenue toward Fresh Pond. Rita was wearing a camel's-hair coat, and Groucho had on his red plaid doggy coat. My parka was navy blue, a color that prominently displays even a single dog hair, and the insulating material and liner were hanging out of the tear Kimi had made in the sleeve, but I didn't feel too shabby to walk with Rita and Groucho. Rowdy was with me. His God-given, Eukanuba-fed coat would have outshone ermine robes. Kimi's would have, too, but since she wasn't civilized enough to go for a stroll with two other dogs, she'd had to stay home.

"I wouldn't want to ask you to violate your ethical standards," I said.

She nodded.

"In fact, I'd rather die."

She rolled her eyes a little, shook her head, and smiled.

"I'm half serious."

I told her the story. A lot of people might have dismissed it. Rita dismisses nothing.

"Look. You think Cambridge is a small world," she said. "You don't even begin to know how small. The therapy network here is incredible. Absolutely everyone's been in treatment or supervision or whatever with everyone else."

"The dog world is the same way," I said. "Everyone knows everyone."

"It's so inbred."

"So are most dogs."

"Cut it out. Look, I can tell you a little about my part, but you have to keep it totally to yourself. You say nothing to anyone. Not to Kevin. Not to anyone."

"Fine. So she was a patient of yours?"

"No. Not really. I saw her twice. It was for an evaluation. I didn't have time myself, and I referred her. I've thought about that a whole lot lately."

"Because?"

"Because apparently it wasn't a good referral."

"What does that mean?"

"That it didn't work out. But . . ."

"You sent her to Elaine Walsh?"

"No. I sent her to a guy named Joel Baker. You know I'm not in the habit of making careless referrals, and I gave that one a whole lot of thought. She needed someone really good. Yeah, who doesn't? But she wouldn't have been easy, and she needed someone very experienced, and someone who'd stay with her when it got rough, because it was going to. And I worked on the referral. I talked it over with Joel. One thing that's bothering me is that when it didn't work out, she didn't come back to me. I told her that if she and Joel thought it wasn't working out, to come back. But she didn't."

"So what was wrong with him?"

"Nothing. It doesn't mean there was anything wrong with him. Maybe they just didn't connect. Or maybe it was a mistake to send her to a man. But I didn't do that thoughtlessly. Besides, Joel is a very unusual man. Of all the male therapists in this city, he probably has the best rep with women for being sensitive to women's issues. I've always thought he was a first-rate therapist."

"So if they just didn't connect, what makes you think it was a bad referral? That wasn't your fault."

"I know. When you make a referral, you aren't making any promise that this is going to be the perfect match. And since she didn't come back to me, that doesn't say a whole lot for the alliance I formed with her, either. I know all that. But . . . Look, this is totally confidential."

"Of course."

"I heard something. Just a rumor. Nothing, really. But it gave me second thoughts. That's all. I won't repeat it, so don't ask me."

I didn't. "Joel Baker. Is he a psychiatrist? An M.D.?"

"Ph.D. psychologist. Actually, you probably know him. They have those big dogs. Hatchbacks."

"Try again."

"Whatever you call them. Razorbacks."

"Ridgebacks. Rhodesian Ridgebacks. He's a kind of slim guy, forty or so? With blond hair. Curly. And a kind of prep school voice."

"What's that supposed to mean?" she asked. "That he didn't go to your high school? Come on, Groucho. Let's move along."

We turned around and headed back up Concord toward home. Rita wears Joan and David boots with heels, and if she walks more than half a mile, her feet hurt, I think, but she always says that Groucho's had it and needs to go home. It wasn't a great day for a walk, anyhow. The temperature was up to forty or so, but the sky was a low, solid gray cloud, and it looked like rain.

"That he didn't go to anyone's high school, or that's what he sounds like. You know what I mean."

"Educated."

"No, not really. Because Cambridge is filled with educated guys who don't talk like that."

"Affected."

"Sort of. Maybe as if it started out as an affectation, but then after a long time it got to be real. I didn't know what it was when I first got here. This is going to sound prejudiced, but it isn't. When I first got here, I honestly thought that all the men who talked like that were gay. Then I found out they weren't. Don't give me that look. Men don't talk like that in Maine. Even gay men don't. Nobody does. I'd never heard it before. Anyhow, Joel and Kelly, right? They live in Cambridge. I didn't know their last name."

"If you've remembered their names and forgotten the names of the dogs, it's a first."

"Nip and Tuck. Sorry to disappoint you. Those are really gorgeous dogs. They show them in breed, you know. They're in great condition. She walks them all the time. I see her around. I guess she doesn't work."

"Holly! Jesus. You are a veritable cauldron of reactionary soup today."

"Outside the home."

"There are women in Cambridge who'd murder you for that. And how do you know? That's probably what she thinks when she sees you."

"Everyone thinks that writers don't work. Anyway, speaking of which, I have a column due that I haven't started. Maybe I'll do something on Ridgebacks."

"No."

"Ridgebacks are a perfectly normal thing to write about if you write for *Dog's Life*. I don't think I've mentioned them lately, and if I don't, I'll get a million letters from the Ridgeback people complaining that the breed has been slighted."

"Sure."

"And I won't actually write anything about the people."

"Do you ever?"

"Sometimes I try, but Bonnie edits it out."

Rita yanked Groucho away from the discarded remains of a submarine sandwich embedded in a pile of dirty, melting ice. Rowdy went for it, too.

"No!" I told him loudly. "Leave it!"

"What's with you?" Rita said. "You don't usually shriek at him like that. It's probably starting to rot, but there's nothing else wrong with it. Do you honestly think that it's poisoned?"

"No. Not really. No. But I don't want him eating it, anyway. Crazy people do go around poisoning dogs, you know."

"You're hedging."

"I'm not. It happens. It happened at a show in the Midwest not all that long ago, to a malamute. He was poisoned at a show. Storm Kloud's Better Than Ever. He was called Luke. He was one of the top-rated malamutes in the country, and he was poisoned. He died."

"That's horrible."

"Of course it's horrible. I cried when I heard about it. I sent a check. There's a fund, the Luke Fund, to give a reward for information about who poisoned him. You see, it does happen. It really could happen here."

Rita shrugged. "This isn't a dog show."

"All the world's a dog show."

"And all the men and women merely terriers, malamutes, dachshunds . . ."

"Enough," I said. "Look, can you tell me one thing? When you saw Donna Zalewski, did she mention dogs?"

Rita shook her head at me.

"How much did she know about dogs? Could she have let

Kimi run loose? Could Kimi have got into some kind of trouble?"

"Holly."

"All right. It's just that Kimi is not the best-behaved dog in the world. She's young. She's still half puppy. I've wondered if she might've done something, got someone furious, someone who didn't understand dogs. Someone who got some kind of pathological hatred for her. Yeah, okay. I guess I can find out for myself."

Chapter 8

WHEN the four of us had returned home and Rita was in her kitchen making coffee, I waited in her living room and checked the Rolodex next to the phone on her desk. I knew that in addition to the phone numbers of her friends, she kept the phone numbers of her patients there in case she got sick or we had a blizzard and she needed to cancel her appointments. Not just phone numbers, it turned out. Addresses, too. Donna Zalewski had lived on Lakeview Avenue. Rita, forgive me. I had to know.

The next morning, I put a metal training collar and a sturdy webbed leash on Kimi and walked her toward what had once been home for her. Lakeview is closer to Fresh Pond than is Appleton Street. The Brattle Street ends of Appleton and Lakeview are inhabited by elderly professors with inherited money and by youthful celebrities, doctors, lawyers, and business people whose social aspirations have taken an intellectual turn. Most of the houses are tall, wide colonials and even taller and wider Victorians with fanciful turrets and room-size wisteria arbors. The opposite ends of Appleton and Lakeview, the ends on my side of Huron Avenue, must originally have provided walk-to-work housing for the Brattle and off-Brattle live-out help, but these days those humbler dwellings, triple-deckers and styleless twenty-room arks, are considered just as intellectual as the Brattle-end mansions but politically correct as well, even after an architect has transformed them. In other words, the neighbors are not just doctors, lawyers, professors, and therapists, but writers, teachers, plumbers, electricians, and cops.

Donna Zalewski had lived in a nondescript brown-shingled

house in the transition zone, barely on the Brattle Street side of Lakeview, just beyond Huron Avenue. The house had a front lawn, or what the winter had left of one, and a cream-colored porch with three mailboxes and no milk box, at least that I could see. There might be one at the back door, I realized, or it could have been removed after Donna's death, if she'd ever had one at all. Kimi briefly lifted her leg on the trunk of a maple in front of the house, but didn't give any sign of recognizing the neighborhood.

"Nice dog," said a burly young guy walking by. "What kind is he?"

"She. A malamute."

"Thought he was some kind of husky."

"She's all malamute," I said.

"Big guy."

"Yes, she is," I said. "She weighs about seventy-five pounds."

"Big feller," he said.

Perhaps I should add that in addition to looking big and strong, Kimi looked feminine. She was not what's known as a doggy bitch. I wouldn't have dared to use that phrase in front of Elaine Walsh. (There are also bitchy dogs, but that probably doesn't even the score.) Anyway, when the guy started to pat Kimi's head, she dropped smartly to the damp concrete sidewalk, rolled onto her back, tucked in her paws, and looked up at him, pleading for a tummy rub. I was happy to see her do it. The alternative was jumping on people, which she'd done a few times. But this dope, who, of course, didn't understand anything about malamutes, stood there looking at her with an embarrassed expression on his face. Obviously, he also had the opportunity to observe that she was a bitch, but it didn't seem to sink in.

"Take it easy, big guy," he said.

When he'd gone on his way, I spent another couple of seconds looking at Donna's house and then walked Kimi toward Brattle. Near Donna's was a house I'd noticed before while walking Rowdy, an ordinary box-shaped brick house with an extraordinary array of plants and stones in front, where you'd expect a lawn. There were six or eight small pink quartz boulders, dozens of upright slabs of granite and slate, and what appeared to be a collection of deformed miniature evergreens and

twisted, grotesquely stunted deciduous trees that had dropped
their leaves and looked as if they'd died painfully. Standing
there staring at it, I felt like the ghouls who slow down for
glimpses of gore at the scene of a highway accident. I was so
taken that I ignored Kimi, who was pawing and sniffing at the
low wall of rough stones around the garden, if you can call it
that, until she treated me like a sled frozen in the ice, almost
tearing my left arm out of its socket and nearly throwing me
to the ground and hauling me up the street toward her goal,
two Rhodesian Ridgebacks and, incidentally, at least from
Kimi's perspective, Kelly Baker, who'd once told me that she
walked those dogs a minimum of six miles a day.

Then Kimi hit the ground. If you're ever walking a malamute and find that at the sight of other dogs, she suddenly
drops to the sidewalk, don't assume that she's spontaneously
put herself on an obedient long down. There's nothing one-
down about that immobile, catlike pose. In wolves, it's called
an ambush. Crouched flat, she's preparing to spring at her prey,
and if you aren't careful, she'll take you along. I should add
that Kimi's ambush posture was like those mock jabs to the
stomach that human male jocks use to greet one another, not
an announcement of a serious wish to start a fight with the
Ridgebacks, Nip and Tuck. Kelly, who probably recognized
the ritual display for what it was and, in any case, knew that
I could handle a dog, didn't panic the way some fools do when
an essentially gentle, friendly creature like Kimi is only pretending to be ferocious. And I can handle a big dog, of course.
You have to relax every muscle in your body and keep all your
joints flexed, especially your hips, knees, ankles, shoulders, elbows, and wrists. In other words, adopt the stance of a Japanese
wrestler, and hang on to the leash with both hands. It worked,
and Elaine Walsh would have been proud of me because I
didn't look at all ladylike. Kimi didn't even come close to
wresting the leash from my hands, and she didn't drag me an
inch toward the Ridgebacks.

"Now, behave yourself," I told her as I hauled in the lead
and stared directly into her eyes. "No more of that. Be a good
girl."

Rhodesian Ridgebacks are big, handsome dogs with short,
sleek coats. The breed ranges in color from a light fawn to a
reddish wheaten. The Ridgeback people will probably hate me

for this, because no other breed really resembles the Ridgeback, but if you've never seen one, imagine a very small, fawn-colored Great Dane, maybe sixty-five or seventy-five pounds, with uncropped ears. The ridge? That's what's unique. Along the backbone of a Ridgeback, a narrow strip of fur grows in the direction opposite to the rest of the coat. Above the shoulders, the ridge makes two swirls—crowns, they're called—that are supposed to be perfectly symmetrical, as they were on Nip and Tuck, who were an identical glossy wheaten red. Nip was the dog; Tuck, the bitch.

"I'll be damned," Kelly greeted me. Flanked by her big dogs, she looked even shorter than she was, and, offering an ever-welcome instance of Winter's rule (that dogs and their owners look nothing alike), had short, very curly, very feminine black hair, like an untrimmed poodle's. "That's Kimi, isn't it?"

I gave Kimi a bit of leash, then all six feet, and the three dogs nosed and smelled each other. Whenever I'd seen Kelly with the Ridgebacks, Tuck, the bitch, had been on leash. Although Nip usually wandered with them off leash, he never seemed to stray far. Today he checked out Kimi's scent, circled around the two bitches, and then devoted himself to a rapt examination of the olfactory history other dogs had inscribed at the base of a nearby maple. When the canine introductions were over, Kimi turned her attention to Kelly, but since I suspected that Kimi would soon start sniffing somewhere that even a dog lover wouldn't appreciate, I hauled her toward me again.

"Yeah, this is Kimi all right," I said. "You know her?"

"Sure. I haven't seen her for a while, but I thought that's who she was. She's a lot bigger now. You want some advice?"

Dog people are always handing out free advice. They'll tell you what breed of dog you want, where to buy him, what to feed him, how to groom, train, and handle him, what judges to show him under, and what to wear yourself when you do. I expected to be told to trade Kimi in for a Ridgeback, or to add canned squash to her dog food, or to use a pinch collar on her, but Kelly surprised me.

"If I were you, I'd keep her away from that rock garden," Kelly said. "You probably noticed it."

"Rock garden. So that's what it's called," I said. We both grinned. "It's really bizarre."

"Joel calls it the garden of death." She smiled. "He has some elaborate theory about the symbolism, how it represents a cemetery. The rocks are all gravestones. And the plants are bodies. And skeletons."

"I guess I can see that. There *is* something sinister about it."

"Anyhow," Kelly said, "the woman just slaves over it. Misguidedly, but she does. And the big problem seems to be that she uses a lot of manure, and it attracts dogs. So, of course, they leave their scent, and that attracts other dogs, and the whole thing escalates."

"Dog heaven."

"Exactly. Anyway, she loathes dogs, and it's remotely possible that she'd remember Kimi. She won't do anything worse than come out and scream at you, but she can be pretty unpleasant."

"What did Kimi do?"

"Got loose a couple of times and started digging."

"And got caught."

"And got caught. And the woman was off the wall about it. Maybe she wouldn't recognize Kimi, anyway, though. She probably thinks all dogs look alike. And Kimi's grown."

"Who is she? The woman."

"Someone with a black thumb who hates dogs. Actually, her name is Green, ironically enough. Anyway, it's her own fault. She's the one who spreads the manure. And she's been told about that, that she ought to switch to something else, but she won't listen."

"Did you know Kimi's first owner?" I didn't mention that I was the third, not the second.

"No," Kelly said. "I mean, I knew what she looked like. That's all."

Kelly thereby proved herself a real dog person, I concluded. She'd remembered Kimi's name and probably never even bothered to find out the name of her owner.

"You knew she died?" I said.

"Really? She was young."

"Yes." There was a moment of silence, as if we were paying respects.

"So what are you up to these days?" Kelly was obviously asking what was going on with my dogs.

"Rowdy and I are training for Open. Kimi's getting a course on basic civilization, and then we'll see."

"That was a good column on submissive urination," she said.

"Thanks," I said. "Actually, I could use your help with one I'm working on now. I was thinking of something about Ridgebacks in obedience. One of the things I like to do is encourage people to get a bigger variety of breeds in obedience."

"So it doesn't look like a breed ring for goldens."

"Right," I said. The American Kennel Club started awarding the O.T.Ch. title, Obedience Trial Champion, in 1977. The first three O.T.Ch. dogs were all golden retrievers. You also see a lot of shelties, Rottweilers, German shepherds, and poodles in obedience, not only because there are a lot of them but because they're good obedience dogs. But you don't see many Ridgebacks in obedience mainly because you don't see many of them anywhere. It's not a common breed. "You got a C.D. with a Ridgeback, didn't you?" I asked Kelly.

"Zing. We co-owned him. And I'm working with these two now. We don't train with Cambridge," she said apologetically.

That's where I train, Cambridge Dog Training Club.

"That's okay." I smiled. "Would you talk to me about it sometime?"

"Sure. You free this afternoon?"

The Bakers' architect-redesigned house at the Fresh Pond end of Lakeview was, like Elaine Walsh's house, a pale yellow, one of the hues made fashionable by the Brattle Street residents who paint their Victorian and colonial mansions—or, should I say, have them painted—in oddly attractive shades of mauvebrown or off-lavender or nonstandard yellow. The Bakers' yellow was creamier than Elaine's, paler and warmer, and they'd succeeded in making the house look both cozy and stylish, outside and inside.

The kitchen had a granite island in the middle, cherry counters with marble splash boards, and a professional, restaurant-size gas range. The counters held a Cuisinart, blue pottery pots filled with metal ladles and wooden spoons, a fully loaded, oversize knife-storage block, and one of those mechanical orange squeezers that cost three times as much as the electric ones, not to mention a four-slice toaster and a Kitchen-Aid appliance big enough to serve as a concrete mixer. You could have cooled my entire kitchen in the built-in refrigerator from which Kelly removed a bottle of milk. Held by a magnet to the refrig-

erator door was a sheaf of papers on a metal clip. A matching
sheaf of papers hung from the door of what must have been
a nearly walk-in freezer. The papers showed neatly printed lists
of the contents of the refrigerator and freezer, by category.
Under the heading "Baked Goods" on the freezer's list were
ladyfingers, madeleines, baguettes, génoise, croissants, and
some other things with French names that I didn't recognize,
and with each item was a notation of an amount and a date.
Some of the amounts had been changed, and some items had
been crossed out. Three quarts of fish stock remained of the
original six in the freezer. The Bakers were down to only a
dozen eggs in the refrigerator.

"I cook," Kelly said. "Not professionally. It's a hobby."

Her blue-flowered pinafore could have passed as an unusu-
ally pretty apron designed for a TV chef with a tendency to
spill everything all over herself. She had the clear, smooth,
translucent skin and bright pink cheeks you see on people who
work in bakeries, but her complexion was probably attributable
to daily marathon dog-walking.

"It looks like more than a hobby," I said.

"I half wish it were. It would give me something to say when
people ask what I do." She grimaced.

"You get a lot of that?"

"In Cambridge? Are you kidding? Try explaining that you
have a traditional marriage around here, and what you see on
people's lips is one word, and that's *victim.*"

She probably didn't realize that it is, in fact, possible to make
coffee without grinding the beans yourself. When I asked where
the chocolate croissants had come from, she said that actually
they were *petits pains au chocolat,* not croissants—they weren't
shaped like crescents—and confessed that she'd made them. I
ate four, including the crumbs, which were buttery flakes, not
crumbs.

I wanted to ask her whether her husband had ever talked
about Donna Zalewski, what had gone wrong between them,
what the rumor about him was that Rita wouldn't pass on,
whether she'd known that Kimi's owner had been her husband's patient, and a lot of other things, but I was distracted.
Besides, the questions would have been tricky to slip in with
the ones I had to ask about Rhodesian Ridgebacks.

"These two are young," she said. "We finished Nip last summer, and we just finished Tuck in December. Joel handles her. He has less time than I do."

Finishing a dog may sound like ending him—another one of those horrible euphemisms—but it means something good: getting a championship in breed, which requires accumulating points at AKC shows. You need fifteen points won under a minimum of three different judges and at least two majors, which are three-, four-, or five-point wins. Championship points go to Winner's Dog and Winner's Bitch (although for some reason I've never understood, the AKC always omits the apostrophes), and . . . And if you don't already know the rest, don't ask.

"Congratulations," I said, and added, referring to Tuck, who, with Nip, was asleep on the floor, "Are you planning to become parents?"

Tuck was a beautiful bitch who'd completed her championship. Kelly was a real dog person. She knew that I was, too. For all I knew, the Bakers had five children. Anyone would have assumed that the Bakers were thinking about breeding Tuck, and Kelly should have assumed that that's what I meant. She didn't. She almost choked on her *petit pain*. Her face fell, and her eyes teared up.

"Kelly, I'm so sorry. Look, I meant Tuck. I meant four-legged parents. I'm so sorry. I'd never have—"

She interrupted me. "Please. Of course. I've gotten hypersensitive about it. Damn. I hear it in anything. It wasn't you. Naturally you meant Tuck. This fertility problem has been so awful. It's such a struggle. And you're right. We *are* planning to become four-legged parents, we hope."

When she pulled a tissue from one of the patch pockets on the front of the pinafore, I realized that it wasn't so much an all-encompassing apron as it was a maternity dress.

"Hell," she said. "Let's talk about dogs."

We talked about Pearsall, which isn't some rare dog breed, but the last name of Milo and Margaret, who revolutionized American dog training. Their book is subtitled "Obedience from the Dog's Point of View," and if dogs got to pick their handlers' training systems, we'd probably all use nothing but Pearsall. I don't think that all of the Pearsalls' step-by-step procedures and all of their barriers, gadgets, and gimmicks are necessary for a smart dog, but I love their attitude. Kelly Baker, though, was a Pearsall fanatic. We talked for a long time.

Joel walked in just as I was finally leaving. He gave me a warm smile, kissed Kelly, and heard about my proposed column on Ridgebacks. I liked him and wondered why Donna Zalewski hadn't. He was only about five five, but next to Kelly, who couldn't have been more than five one, he looked tall. Although by the standards of my rural Maine background, his blond hair was too well cut, his face too smoothly shaven, and his mouth too close to pretty, he could certainly be considered an attractive man. I remembered something I'd read in that feminist book Elaine Walsh had given me, something about men feeling most like men when women are clearly and unambiguously women, and I wondered whether that was what had attracted Joel to Kelly. As the book suggested, maybe her petite femininity made him feel masculine, and maybe he felt most like a man when he was out working and she was home in that wonderful kitchen. Elaine Walsh had told me that all marriage is slavery, but that wasn't the feeling I had about the Bakers' marriage, which I knew must have been tried by the fertility problem. I felt even worse than I had before about my blunder.

There was no mystery about Kimi's origin. She'd done some minor damage and irked an evidently harmless and eccentric dog hater. When she belonged to Elaine Walsh, she'd hardly been taken beyond the front walk, so she hadn't had much opportunity to enrage anyone. Donna Zalewski might or might not have had a milkman, and I'd discovered nothing about anything she might have said to Joel Baker, nothing about Kimi, nothing about Donna herself. I was beginning to conclude that Kimi hadn't been anyone's intended victim. I thought that I'd mostly spent my time making Kelly feel bad and that I hadn't learned anything. But, maybe because I was still stuck on that damned reincarnation story, I couldn't shake the sense that Kimi was somehow involved, that she knew something, had done something, or could tell me something. I didn't know what.

Chapter 9

"So tell me about Sinequan," I said.

Rita and I were at my kitchen table sharing one of nature's perfect foods: pizza. Cheese? Dairy group. Crust? Grains. Tomatoes, anchovies . . . If you order right, you hit all those food groups we learned about in junior high. It's practically human Eukanuba, and if you avoid hot peppers, dogs like it, too. On a long down on the linoleum, Rowdy looked up at us, wide-eyed but motionless. In deference to Rita, Kimi was locked in her crate in my bedroom.

"You don't hear about it much anymore," Rita said. "It isn't trendy, you know? Since Valium came out, you practically never hear about Librium, and Valium isn't really trendy because anxiety is *démodé* at the moment."

Rita, unlike certain prescription drugs, never goes out of style. She'd quit perming, scrunching, and messing up her hair a while ago and now had it in a short, straight cut that had to be trimmed every two weeks but was worth the bother because it didn't make her look like an ungroomed puli with a bald face. She looks as if she'd eat pizza with a knife and fork, but she uses her hands like everyone else.

"And what's *à la mode?*"

"Depression," she said cheerfully. "Prozac." She rolled the word out and repeated it. "Prozac."

Even I had heard of Prozac. You couldn't go to a party in Cambridge without having to listen to six or eight people tell you how much better they were feeling since they'd been on it.

"Doesn't that cut into your business?" I asked. Rita isn't an M.D. She does talking cures.

"Not really. It doesn't help everyone. And people don't take it forever. And a lot of people who feel helped, in the sense that they're less depressed, still don't like it because they don't feel like themselves when they're taking it. Maybe they don't when they're not, either."

"That's how I felt after Vinnie died. Before I got Rowdy." Vinnie was my last golden, a gift from my mother. And the gods. "Without a dog, I just wasn't myself."

"Really! Some of these people already have dogs."

"Like Donna Zalewski. She did."

"No." She studied the half-eaten wedge in her hand. A mushroom dangled from a string of mozzarella. She fixed her eyes on it and observed its motion as if the pizza slice were one of her patients and the mushroom a facial tic she was about to interpret.

"Did I ask you anything? I said she had a dog. Kimi."

Rita made a face.

"I just want to ask one thing, and it isn't about her. Listen. Where would somebody get something like Sinequan? Joel Baker's not a psychiatrist, right? He can't prescribe? And Elaine Walsh couldn't, either."

"Joel's a Ph.D. psychologist."

"Like Elaine. Right? Like you."

"Yes."

"So, just theoretically, suppose you've got a patient, and she can't sleep or something and wants a prescription, what do you do?"

"Talk about it," Rita said.

"Come on. Therapists aren't supposed to be moralistic, right? Suppose somebody wants Prozac. Just imagine that for once you decide that maybe it's a good idea. Or something is. Couldn't that happen?"

"Of course. It does."

"Okay. So what do you do? Do you call up the person's regular doctor?"

"No. You make a referral to somebody who does meds. Any M.D. can write the prescription, and lots of people get Prozac or Valium or whatever from their internists or G.P.'s and never see a therapist at all. Sometimes that's part of the problem you're dealing with. It isn't hard to get a prescription. You just don't happen to know that because you never go to a doctor."

"That's not true."

"Vets don't count. Anyway, I've had people come to me, and I've taken them on and started work with them before I found out they were taking Valium and Seconal, Ativan, Xanax. There's this real bastard named Arsenault. People go to him, and he gives them whatever they want. The original Dr. Feelgood."

"A psychiatrist?"

"An asshole."

"By training?"

"By birth. He's a G.P. or something. His office is in Arlington. Fortunately, there aren't too many like him. You know, doing meds is a fine art, really, when it's done right, when it's done carefully. There are people who specialize in it and people who for whatever reason have a special interest in it. And, by the way, I'm not moralistic. There are people who need to be on medication and who are helped by it. There are people who can't function otherwise."

"So if you get somebody like that, what do you do? Is there somebody you send people to?"

"Yeah. Well, it depends. If it's some minor, transitional thing, sometimes I send people to Ben Moss. Otherwise, there's a woman in Brookline who's been very helpful to people I've sent."

"Ben Moss. He's the one who prescribed Sinequan for Donna Zalewski. Kevin told me that."

"So if you know that, what are you trying to pump me for?"

"Okay, Rowdy," I said. That's his release word. He jumped to his feet. "Catch." He loves pizza crust and has incredible eye-mouth coordination. He never misses. I tore a piece of crust into bits and kept tossing them in the air, and he kept snapping them in his jaws, one after the other. "I want to know who Ben Moss is. And whether you sent Donna Zalewski to him."

"You probably know who he is," Rita said. "They have a dog."

"You may find this hard to believe, but I really don't know absolutely every person who owns a dog. There are more than fifty million dogs in this country. I can't remember how many owners there are . . ."

"Naturally."

"But how could I know all of them? Rowdy, catch."

"The Mosses' dog is another one of those hatchbacks, like the ones the Bakers have."

"Ridgebacks. Rhodesian Ridgebacks," I said. See what's wrong with human education? How could a supposedly educated person forget something like that? "African lion hounds. That's another name for them. Rhodesian Ridgebacks."

"Shouldn't it be Zimbabwe?"

"Would you like to explain that to the American Kennel Club? You want to know how progressive the AKC is? They wouldn't accept women delegates until 1974. The Ladies' Dog Club had to send a man. You think that's cute? I didn't make it up. It's true. And if you'd ever tried to get them to change a dog's name . . ."

"I haven't."

"Well, if you had, you'd forget about asking them to change the name of a breed. Even if you succeeded, you'd be dead by the time the change went into effect. Besides, a lot of dog people aren't political." Except about American Kennel Club politics, of course. "So what does the dog look like?"

"Big," Rita said emphatically. "Have you ever noticed that you hardly ever ask what people look like? When you want to identify people, you ask what their dogs look like. There happens to be a whole universe of people out there who think all dogs look pretty much alike, you know."

"It must be a universe of fools," I said. "Is this an oversize male Ridgeback? Tall? A little rangy and leggy? Kind of a brownish-tan wheaten color. Not much red. Can I give your crust to Rowdy?"

She nodded.

"But with a nice ridge and good crowns," I added.

"That's the one," she said. "Fabulous dental work. Great bonding and sealing. Flashy smile."

"Now who's getting cute? Anyway, as a matter of fact, I do know that dog, I think. And if it's the one I think it is, it's a very sweet dog. And it does smile. The woman is maybe in her early forties, with long hair? And long skirts. Birkenstock sandals in winter, with socks, right?"

"Sheila Moss," Rita said. "She's a social worker."

"So tell me about Ben Moss. Sorry, buddy, it's all gone."

An intelligent dog is easier to own than a stupid dog, most of the time. Rowdy had had his eye on the pizza from the second we'd opened the box, and he knew I was telling the truth. He'd monitored the exact amount that had gone into our mouths and his. A stupid dog might have thought I was holding out on him and pestered for more, but not Rowdy.

"Ben Moss is the co-owner of the dog," Rita said. "Owning a dog constitutes his entire identity. What else could you possibly want to know about him?"

"Stop it. I don't think I know him. I only know the dog because she had him in our beginners' class for a while, and I noticed him. I like Ridgebacks. You see a few of them in obedience, but not many. I didn't even know she was married. You think if I know her, I know him? She's just some extension of her husband? What would Elaine have said about that?"

"Actually, I assumed that if you knew the dog . . ."

"Rita, please. I cannot understand why you are doing this. Donna Zalewski was sort of a client of yours."

It's hard to decide whether to say *patient* or *client* to Rita. Sometimes she says *patient* herself, but if I do, she looks offended. The problem, I guess, is that *client* sounds like *customer,* as if she ran a store or cut their hair. *Consumer* is impossible, of course. Rita isn't some new brand of ketchup or a household appliance. One time when I asked her whether they were patients or clients, she said that it depended on how sick they were, but later she said to forget it, that it was serious and she shouldn't have been flip.

"And," I added, "Elaine was a friend of yours, too."

"I knew Elaine," she said. "We were in a group together. And I really am sorry about what happened to her. But look. You've already gone and upset Kelly Baker. The next thing you're going to do is visit the Mosses and tell them that you want an interview with their dog. Correct? You'll make it a star? It'll end up in *Dog's Life?*"

"So to speak."

"Well, reopening one wound was enough. If you talk to Sheila Moss, do not, I repeat, *do not* mention Elaine Walsh."

"You want to tell me why not?"

"No, as a matter of fact, I don't."

"Then I have no reason not to mention Elaine, do I?"

"Yes, you do. Your reason is that I'm asking you not to."

"And after I don't, you pat me on the head and tell me what a good girl I am?"

"Holly, you don't want to. Would you just take my word for it? There's a relationship there that you don't know about. You don't like hurting people."

"So was she a patient of Elaine's?"

"No. Holly . . ."

"Rita, if she and Elaine were very close, it probably consoles her to have people talk about Elaine. After you lose someone you care about, you need to hear that other people are mourning, too. And if they had some kind of, uh, special relationship, I don't care. I mean, I'm not as provincial as you like to think. I know she didn't believe in bourgeois taboos that exclude—"

Rita interrupted me. "Look, Elaine was not having an affair with Sheila. She was doing something much more bourgeois than that. She was having an affair with Ben. She probably didn't call it that. I don't know what she called it." Rita stretched her neck and looked up at the ceiling as if Elaine's voice might come from beyond to provide her with the right phrase. It didn't.

"Elaine told me she didn't believe in marriage. Maybe she really, really didn't believe in marriage."

"Did she ever talk to you about sisterhood?" Rita looked angry.

"Not much."

"She made me want to throw up when she did," Rita said. "But, of course, she was less voluble about it lately. It's gone out of style."

"Did Sheila Moss know about Elaine?"

"I've never asked her," Rita said. "Don't you."

"Does Kevin know?"

"I haven't asked him, either."

After Rita left, when I let Kimi loose, I felt guilty. Rowdy had eaten all the pizza crust, and it had never occurred to me to save any for Kimi.

"You really are my dog, too," I assured her. "I'm sorry I forgot."

Then I phoned Steve.

"It's Holly. Something is bothering me. It's stupid, but I need to ask."

"With Kimi? It's normal for her to lift her leg like that, you know. She's a nice, healthy bitch."

"I know that," I said.

"You'll see shepherds do it, too. Lots of breeds."

"I know!"

"What's the problem?"

"I'm just going to spit this out. Okay? It's probably nothing. Look, Elaine Walsh didn't believe in marriage. In fact, I just looked it up in one of her books, and what she said is that she didn't acknowledge marriage. On the grounds that it's a form of slavery. If you acknowledge it, you condone it."

"What are you talking about?"

"I mean, if she didn't acknowledge marriage, she'd hardly think the vet-owner relationship was sacred, would she?"

"You don't."

"Oh, yes, I do. That's exactly what I think. But my world-view is a little different from Elaine's. What's sacred to me might have been profane to her. And vice versa."

"You want to know if Elaine seduced me?"

"No," I said. "Did she act interested?"

"No," he said. "And I wouldn't have been interested if she had. You know that." His voice turned scornful. "Even if it hadn't been for you, I wouldn't have been interested. The woman was a philistine."

He didn't have to elaborate. He meant that she didn't know the first thing about dogs.

Shortly after I hung up, as I was standing at the sink washing human plates and dog bowls and working out a feminist perspective on jealousy, I heard one of those sounds I know so well, the bang of a plastic plant mister hitting the kitchen floor, immediately followed by the jangling crash of a metal can that had once held coffee and now contained a handful of noisy pennies. Since Kimi's arrival, the wastebasket lid had been densely covered with dog deterrents, but malamutes don't scare easily. I heard the rapid rustle and furtive swish of a dog raiding the trash. By the time I turned my head, Kimi was a blurred gray streak dashing toward my bedroom door, a streak carrying an oil-and-cheese-soaked pizza box in its jaws.

I turned off the faucet, dried my hands, and practiced a meditative exercise I learned in a Zen handling seminar. All of my negative thoughts disappeared of their own accord and made mental room for the image of Kimi trotting back to the kitchen and depositing her spoils at my feet. The picture came, but she didn't. I took slow, deliberate steps to the bedroom. She wasn't there, or so it seemed until I heard molars grinding up cardboard in the narrow tunnel formed by my platform bed and the wall. Gripping the box in her front paws, she was holed up in the den, gnawing on her prey. Rowdy, who'd followed her into the room, stood in a spot in the middle of the room, debating with himself, I suppose, about whether to steal her kill or enjoy the show. If I failed to come out top dog with Kimi, she wouldn't be the only one to demote me in the pack hierarchy.

"Rowdy, sit," I told him in the same calm tone of voice I always used. He obeyed. "Good boy. Stay."

Kimi had made one mistake. She'd dragged a large carcass into a small den. A corner of the carton projected a few inches. "Kimi, that is mine." I tried to sound matter-of-fact. I reached down, grabbed the carton in both hands to stop it from ripping, and gave it a sharp jerk. I got most of it, and, as I'd optimistically calculated, she was so tightly wedged behind the bed that she couldn't emerge in time to snatch it back. Although I felt tempted to slip the carton out of sight before she freed herself, I stood and held it as I watched her squirm and crawl out. She saw me in possession. So did Rowdy. For now, at least, I was still top dog.

Chapter 10

SINCE Steve Delaney took over from old Dr. Draper, the practice has doubled in size, and about three quarters of the new human clients are women, a phenomenon that Steve cannot understand any more than he can understand the rise in trivial and psychosomatic ailments among the patients he inherited from Dr. Draper. Maybe *psychosomatic* is the wrong word. The psyches involved are human, the somata animal.

"Why would anyone pay me to trim a cat's nails?" he'll complain. "I've shown her how to do it, and I've watched her. I'm not a damned manicurist. And there's that lunatic who keeps wanting pregnancy tests on that boxer I spayed last year."

Steve's hair is brown, thick, and wavy, like the coat on the shoulders and neck of a Chesapeake Bay retriever. His eyes are greener than Siberian-husky blue and just as intense, but not at all unnerving.

"They aren't doing it intentionally," I tell him. "They just have an urge to be around you."

"It makes me feel like some kind of object when you say that," he'll protest. "It's dehumanizing. I hate it."

"Imagine that," I'll say. "I just can't fathom what it would feel like."

Before Kimi's arrival, we'd been seeing quite a lot of each other and hadn't been having any big problems. Rowdy and Steve's two bitches, India, the German shepherd, and Lady, the pointer, got along well together as long as we fed them separately, and, in fairness to Rowdy, nobody got to sleep in the room with us, even though he was the only one who'd howl. Kimi was still wild—I was working almost exclusively on teaching her to watch me and barely trying to start her heeling and sitting—but, at least in the absence of food, she and Rowdy were beginning to work things out. With either India or Lady, though, she was a fiend, leaping on the other bitch, snarling, provoking wrath in India and terror in Lady, who would barricade herself behind Steve and whimper to him.

"Why the hell doesn't he just leave the dogs home?" Rita said when I explained the problem to her.

"India doesn't understand, and Lady needs him."

"Don't you?"

"No. At least not the way India and Lady do."

Even so, he arrived without them at about nine, not long after I'd taken the pizza carton away from Kimi, and we had a longer talk than we'd managed on the phone or could have had with all four dogs around.

"So," I said as we sat on the living room floor—still no rug to go in front of the fireplace, but a great blaze of seasoned Maine white birch—"there's no mystery about Kimi, and if she bothered the neighbors or anything, it wasn't any more than any other dog, really. Also, I'm starting to get a new take on Elaine Walsh, and it's making me wonder whether someone might not have been after *her,* not Kimi. And that would mean someone who didn't know her, or at least someone who didn't know her very well. At least, not—that she didn't like cottage cheese and only bought it for Kimi."

"There is one thing about Kimi." Steve talks slowly and sounds midwestern. He says *yerp* for *Europe.* When he talks about a "whore movie" he means something with a monster in it, not a prostitute.

My great pizza victory had left Kimi calm and happy. She was sprawled on the floor next to him with one of her forepaws in his hand. He was rubbing the fingers of his other hand gently and slowly up and down the bar of black fur that ran from the cap on her head down to her nose and tracing the black fur goggles around her eyes. "It's . . . Look. A couple of times when I first saw her, she had this odd thing. Patches of fur missing. Just small patches, almost bald. Like she'd lost a chunk of fur, in a fight maybe."

"I don't understand."

"I didn't, either. I still don't."

"Hot spots?"

Hot spots are areas of red, wet skin that usually develop in hot weather. They itch so ferociously that the dog licks and scratches them in a futile search for relief that exacerbates the problem and ruins his coat.

"Nothing like that. Honest to God, it looked to me just like it had been pulled out."

"What did Elaine say about it?"

"This was before Elaine. The other one."

"Donna Zalewski? I didn't know you saw Kimi then."

"Yeah. Anyway, the owner didn't act concerned about it. Sometimes, especially if it's a pretty dog like this one, they'll get all upset if something's wrong with the coat and want you to run every test. Some of them get worried that it's contagious and they'll catch it. And if it's mange, some owners have hysterics. But this wasn't, and whatever it was, it didn't bother the owner."

"But it bothered you."

"Yeah."

"Why? Couldn't it have been an allergy or something? I mean, it cleared up."

"It didn't look like an allergy. And there were no wounds, nothing that looked like she'd been fighting. She hadn't been chewing, according to the owner, and I didn't see her chewing, or scratching. It looked to me like someone had been pulling out clumps of her fur. That's what it looked like to me."

"Abuse?"

He held Kimi's head in his hands. "Sometimes you can't miss it. Sometimes you can't tell at all. But usually, what you see is that the dog's been kicked, or the dog cringes when a hand's anywhere near him. Sometimes you just wonder."

"Did Donna Zalewski seem like . . ."

"I couldn't tell. No, I mean she was one of those people who'd come in with a whole long written list from the breeder. She wasn't out to save money. She wanted everything done right. She knew this was a very dominant bitch, and she knew she had to start obedience training. She knew it was overdue. Things weren't so bad then. That started with the next one. Kimi knew she could take advantage of her. They always know who can be pushed around."

"So she pushed Elaine around. But not Donna Zalewski? At least not so much."

"That's how it seemed to me. I didn't spend a lot of time with them."

"And maybe Donna Zalewski . . ."

"Maybe."

"But why would anyone . . . ? I've never heard of that before."

"Me neither."

Sheila Moss looked the way I remembered her, but older and thinner. The long brown hair that had probably flowed thickly twenty years ago hung thinly, limp and gray-streaked. Her face matched her hair, limp and streaked in brown and gray. Maybe she smeared brown eye shadow on the upper and lower lids. Maybe exhaustion did it for her.

We were sitting on a Haitian cotton couch that must have been white once and probably hadn't come from the store embellished with quite so many streaks of red Magic Marker. A great many oversize pillows were piled here and there on the floor, all covered in Marimekko fabric in patterns I could remember from my childhood, when my mother used to take me to the old Design Research store in Harvard Square. The window shades were Marimekko, too, swirls of primary green and orange fighting to remain cheerful under the dust and through the rusty water stains. On the wall facing the couch hung a long, wide length of fabric stretched on a frame, a blue pattern of onion-shaped domes.

"I'm sorry I didn't have time to pick up after the kids," Sheila said. "My last client was at six, and I didn't get home till seven-thirty, and then I had to drive the baby-sitter."

Of course she hadn't had time to pick up. It would have taken at least a month, and I'd only called that morning. Toys were everywhere—three Big Wheel tricycles, a set of giant orange cardboard blocks, a wooden indoor slide, a green plastic rocking boat, hundreds of bristle blocks, stacking cubes, Cuisenaire rods, peg dolls, natural wood trains and tracks, stuffed bears in all sizes, hardcover picture books, and enough Lego blocks to make a detailed model of New York City. On the battered oak coffee table in front of the couch were arrayed a half-chewed slice of whole-grain toast, a carefully folded disposable diaper (soiled, and not with urine), a chipped pottery teapot with a dirty beige glaze, and two large chipped-to-match blue pottery mugs. Heavy brown baked clay showed in the chips.

"It's fine." I wanted to sound sincere because, in a way, I was. "I haven't picked up after my dogs, either. I really appreciate your finding time to see me."

"I've always been sorry I didn't keep training Id."

That's right. Id. Where but Cambridge? This can be a humiliating city for a dog. Sheila must have read my face.

She apologized. "The name started out as a joke, about how much he sleeps. That he's mostly unconscious? It sounds silly, but it's too late now. Anyway, I liked training him, but it took so much time, and I couldn't manage it."

The Ridgeback, whose name I have trouble repeating, was curled up asleep on the floor with his head on one of the Marimekko pillows. He was even bigger and leggier than I'd remembered him, like a young calf kept as a house pet.

"Lots of people just come for eight weeks or so," I said. "It is time-consuming. And for people who have families and jobs and everything, it can be too much."

"Especially back then," she said. "I was just finishing graduate school, and the children were mostly in diapers."

"All at once?" She'd said she had four children. "You have twins?"

She laughed. "No. Ben feels strongly that toilet training isn't something to rush. That they should come to it in their own time. And they were still tiny. Josh, our oldest, was only three. And I was breast-feeding the baby. Getting the dog then wasn't perfect timing."

"How did you happen to get a Ridgeback?"

"We knew some people who had them, and we wanted a dog who'd be good with children. And he really is. We didn't realize how big he was going to get, but it doesn't matter. He's the gentlest dog I've ever known. He doesn't even fight with other dogs. Sometimes the cat sleeps next to him. We have a cat, too. Adler." It probably meant something I missed. Somewhere, the Mosses also had a litter box. It needed emptying. "And if he notices her, he'll lick her and wash her fur."

"Who were the people? With the Ridgebacks?"

"Kelly and Joel Baker."

Although she'd been talkative and friendly until then and had referred to the Bakers as friends, she didn't have much to say about them, and since I couldn't imagine what aspect of Ridgeback anything my imaginary column was supposed to be about, I had trouble formulating questions about the giant gentleman asleep on the floor.

Before long, I said that I'd better be going. "I've probably kept you up past your bedtime," I apologized.

She laughed. "I haven't even started to cook dinner yet."

It was almost ten o'clock.

"Ben—my husband—likes to eat late. He lived abroad for a couple of years, and he picked up the time schedule. And tonight he has a seminar that lasts until ten. And after I do the dishes, I've really got to give the dog at least a little walk, and then I really ought to work on our billing. Ben's is too much for him. So don't worry. The night is young."

"The Superwoman syndrome," Rita said. "Didn't you recognize it?"

I'd tapped on her door before I'd even gone into my own place.

"Jesus. Four kids. A big dog. Some kind of therapy practice. And the house is falling apart, but it's gigantic. It's like a museum of used stuff from Design Research with a few hundred thousand dollars' worth of new toys dropped all over everything. And at ten o'clock at night, she's going to start cooking for him, and then she's going to do the dishes. And that's not all."

"Superwoman isn't a viable role," Rita said. "It isn't for anyone. Some women manage to create a façade of succeeding with it, but the price they pay is just as high, even if it's less visible."

"If she knew about his affair with Elaine, that would have been a strong motive, I think. After all the work she does? With all she must have to put out? But I really can't understand it. If I found myself in a marriage like that, I wouldn't murder the other woman. I wouldn't wait for him to have an affair. I'd just kill him, I think. What choice would you have? If you wanted to survive?"

"You'd have one or two others," Rita said. "None of them would be easy."

"For a start, I'd like to take at least one or two of those children and give them to the Bakers. And speaking of the Bakers, what's the story there? And don't look at me like that. Elaine's name was never mentioned, and Sheila brought up the Bakers. I didn't. But then she didn't seem to want to say anything about them, even though she said they were friends."

"They know each other. Not that well, I think. She and Kelly used to have lunch," Rita said. "Maybe they don't anymore."

I knew there was something she wasn't saying. "And?"

"And I don't know. What I know is that Ben told Sheila not to refer to Joel Baker anymore. Sheila told me that."

"That's the rumor you heard about him?"

"Yes."

"Well, so what?"

"You don't get it. There's no reason why you should. It's in code, I guess. When I hear that about a male therapist, I don't need to ask why. Sometimes people almost spell it out, anyway. They tell you not to refer women."

"Joel Baker?"

"I didn't ask to hear this, and I don't intend to pass it along. And don't you."

"Of course not. Is it true?"

"How could I possibly know? Sometimes when I hear this about a male therapist, it pretty much just confirms what I've already suspected. Or in a couple of cases, heard from a patient. But Joel? No. I've never heard anything like this before. You know, I'm telling you strictly in confidence. And I have no intention of passing it along to anyone else."

"Are you going to stop sending people to him?"

Rita's face looked pained. "I haven't decided," she said.

"Sheila Moss didn't strike me as a gossip. She doesn't seem malicious."

"Oh, she isn't. Her intention was protective, I'm sure. She just wanted to protect any women who might be hurt."

"I guess she'd know about that. About hurt."

The next morning, I wasted some time with the woman who was refusing to come back to life, at least on paper. Then I finished drafting a column on Canine Good Citizen testing, an AKC program to encourage responsible dog ownership by issuing CGC certificates to dogs that pass the test, which requires ordinary decent behavior, not formal obedience training. My column argued that clubs should support the program. My heart, however, quoted Winifred Gibson Strickland, author of

Expert Obedience Training for Dogs, who says that if something
is worth doing, it's worth doing right. Obedience competition
is an aristocratic meritocracy, and dogs deserve the chance to
earn their titles, especially dogdom's royalty, the Alaskan malamute. (You can't say that in *Dog's Life,* of course.)

It was dark out and close to dinner by the time I'd walked
and trained my prince and princess, and I left them in the pal-
ace while I ran down the block to buy myself some chowder
at the Fishmonger, which is one of a row of three food shops
on Huron Avenue near the corner of Appleton. The fishmonger
herself is so down-to-fish that her establishment transcends
yuppie, and the seafood she sells tastes fresh even to someone
from Owls Head, Maine, who would rather eat dog food than
supermarket fish, and, in fact, once won a bet by doing just that.

When I left the Fishmonger, I found the Bakers' Ridgebacks,
Nip and Tuck, leashed to a lamppost outside. Joel and Kelly
were emerging from the next shop. Snow was beginning to fall.

"All alone?" Kelly asked me.

"They've had their outing," I said, and added, to Joel, "Not
the kind of walk yours get. No wonder they're in such great
shape."

Since Rhodesian Ridgebacks come from Africa, you'd predict that they'd hate a New England winter, but Nip and Tuck
eyed the snowflakes with malamute-like gleams of joy. Red-
brown coats shining, cleanly muscled bodies prancing, they
looked like the foundation stock of some new and improved
breed of reindeer.

"Kelly deserves all the credit for that." Joel sounded proud.
There are some husbands in Cambridge who would have re-
plied that their wives didn't have anything better to do than
walk the dogs.

"It's half self-indulgence," Kelly said.

When I heard the word, I realized that she did look indulged,
or at least cared for. The sleeves and hem of her thick down
parka weren't dog-shredded, and the pockets weren't torn,
probably because, as I noticed when I'd seen her dog-walking,
she owned at least six or eight parkas and could discard any
clothing that the dogs tailored for her. She wore lightweight,
expensive hiking boots, but her feet were so small that the boots
looked pretty, almost dainty. Furthermore, her clothes
matched: red hat, gloves, and scarf, tan everything else. Rita

has reminded me that most people don't exclaim in surprise when they notice that colors they're wearing happen not to clash.

"Ignore her," Joel said. "She hates being out in the freezing rain as much as anyone else."

He looked quite *soigné* himself. His wool topcoat obviously hadn't come from Goodwill, and he didn't need a haircut.

"Right." She smiled. "I'm just a martyr to the dogs."

While I was standing there hoping that the Bakers would invite me to dinner—and while they weren't inviting me—a new Volvo station wagon pulled into the tow zone at the curb next to us. Sheila Moss stepped out. Her coat must have come from Afghanistan or Nepal via one of the ethnic shops in Harvard Square. It was made of some thick, brown burlap-like material patched with bits of leather and fur. In place of buttons, it had elaborately looped frog fasteners, two of which were badly ripped. On her feet were those hideous, rational sandals, worn over thick Ragg wool socks. In any other city in America except possibly Berkeley, California, she'd have been mistaken for an eccentric beggar, but by Cambridge norms, she exuded prosperity.

I somehow had the idea that since Sheila had been telling people not to refer to Joel, she might do something old-fashioned and embarrassing, like cut him dead, or something modern and embarrassing, like confront him with the issue, as Rita would say. All Sheila did, though, was greet Kelly and me first, then Joel, and the Bakers probably didn't even notice.

"Oh, God," Sheila said. "I'm late as usual. And there's nothing to eat in the house except hot dogs for the kids, and that's not exactly Ben's idea of dinner, is it? You know, the tortellini at Formaggio aren't bad, especially the spinach ones. Have you tried them?" She stopped. "What am I saying?" she added nervously. "You don't buy them, do you? You make your own."

"Not very often," Kelly said. "And if I had four children, it'd be never." Her pretty face showed no sign of grief, but she smacked her lips to Tuck and began stroking the Ridgeback's head.

"Speaking of which," Sheila said, "I've got to go and get mine."

I couldn't tell whether she meant the tortellini or her children. Rita is right about trying to be Superwoman, you see. It's impossible to succeed, and if you make the effort, anyway, you risk sounding as if you can't tell your offspring from some lumps of gourmet macaroni. Or maybe that's motherhood.

Chapter 11

EVEN though there's a laundromat only about a block up Concord Avenue from my house, I hired Ron Coughlin, who's my plumber as well as one of my dog-training buddies, to install a coin-op washer and dryer in the basement for my tenants and me. In winter, Cambridge sidewalks develop icy ruts. Between the sidewalks and the streets, hardened mounds of filthy, packed stuff that was once snow form barricades that are no fun to scale when you're carrying a basket of laundry. Since most of Rita's clothes are dry-clean-only (a category in which she places her one pair of jeans), she hardly uses the machines at all, but I do my own laundry, and so did my third-floor tenants at the time, a cat-owning Swiss couple who shared the housework so fifty-fifty that neither would carry laundry up and down stairs or transfer wet clothes from the washer to the dryer without the other's help. They were the ones who heard the key clanging in the dryer, where it must have fallen out of the pocket of the jeans I'd worn the first day I visited Elaine Walsh, and who returned it to me.

The vertical slats still screened the front door of Elaine Walsh's house from the street, and the lock hadn't been changed. Kevin Dennehy had refused to tell me anything about the contents of the files he'd found in Elaine's office, and when I'd asked him to get me a copy of Donna Zalewski's suicide note, he'd fiddled and diddled, as Johnny Most always said in his Celtics play-by-plays.

The police were economizing on Elaine's estate's fuel and cleaning bills. The house was cold and smelled like a refrigerator that hadn't been opened for weeks, and there was a lot of dust, some of it thick gray powder. On the third floor of the

building, which was the second floor of Elaine's house, were
her bedroom, the bed stripped of sheets and a down comforter
tossed on the floor, a white-tiled bath, and the room I was looking for, a small, windowless study that someone other than
Elaine would probably have used as a walk-in closet. In the
study were a small bookshelf, a chair, a Panasonic printer on
a stand, and a desk on which sat a modernistic-looking goose-
neck lamp and a Zeos 286 computer.

The drawers of the desk had been emptied of everything except office junk, pens and pencils, and the police must have
taken any hard copy and diskettes Elaine had had, but they'd
left the computer. If Elaine had realized how badly I needed
a new computer and had foreseen how good I'd be to Kimi,
she'd have bequeathed me the Zeos 286, so I felt justified in
booting it up and scanning the contents of the hard drive. She'd
used WordPerfect, but hadn't locked any of the document files.
I retrieved quite a few. She evidently hadn't used the computer
to store any notes she might have kept on her patients. Many
files seemed to be chapters of a new book. Many were letters.
Two were addressed to Joel Baker. The first was dated a couple
of months earlier.

Dear Dr. Baker:
    In the course of my treatment of a former client of
yours, Ms. Donna Zalewski, serious questions have arisen
about certain ethical matters related to your own conduct
in the relationship between therapist and patient.
    Please meet with me at the above address, my office,
to discuss this very serious matter.

She gave him a date and time and didn't ask whether the appointment was convenient for him.

The second was dated a couple of days before Elaine's death:

Dear Dr. Baker:
    Your failure to respond satisfactorily to my previous
communication, followed by the tragic death of Donna
Zalewski, in combination with the need to prevent future
occurrences of this type, leaves me no option other than
to share the information that has come to my attention

with the appropriate board of the Massachusetts Psychological Association.

    As a matter of professional responsibility, I believe that no client should be left unprepared for revelations about a therapist. For the sake of your clients, then, and in the hope that you will undertake appropriate arrangements, I shall delay my communication to the board for ten days following this letter.

"I understand all about your professional ethics," I said to Rita. "I sympathize. Anyone would. If I went to a therapist, I wouldn't want her to go around talking about me to other people. I wouldn't want anyone to do that even after I died, even if I died a natural death. And I'm not asking you to go public, you know. I'm not Kevin Dennehy. And believe it or not, this isn't the kind of story *Dog's Life* usually publishes. Somehow I don't think they'd be interested."

Rita's left elbow was resting on my kitchen table, and she kept spreading her left hand open like a giant comb and running it through her hair. Her face was pale, and she kept biting her lips. Old nervous habits die hard even after as much therapy as Rita's had.

"I really don't know what to do," she said, picking up the copy of the first letter. I'd printed out both and brought them home. "Apparently, he didn't respond to this, or at least didn't meet with her. I find that hard to understand."

I picked up the copy of the second letter. "This says 'respond satisfactorily.' It sounds to me as if he did respond, but she didn't like what he said. Maybe he just called her and said he didn't do it. If he was innocent, isn't that what he'd have done? Why should he take orders from Elaine and show up when and where she wanted just because she summoned him? That first letter is practically a subpoena. If somebody sent me a letter like that, I'd call as soon as I read it and ask what the hell was going on. Wouldn't you?"

"Yes, but this is different. There really isn't an equivalent, for women. Women therapists simply don't take sexual advantage of male clients. It's one of those things women don't do. Like strangling. Did you know that? I learned it at a conference on gender difference. Men strangle men. Men strangle women. Women don't strangle anyone."

"No one strangled Elaine," I said.

"I can't imagine Joel strangling anyone," Rita said. "Or hurting someone. He's always seemed like such a calm, stable person. He makes such good contact with people. Even the most borderline people tend to feel safe with him. I have a hard time believing any of this, especially about Joel. I have always had the highest regard for him. Sheila was one thing, but this is so . . . Obviously, Donna made this accusation to Elaine, and Elaine passed it along to Ben. Then Ben told Sheila, and Sheila told me and God knows who else. So it wasn't just Sheila fantasizing . . ."

"Maybe it's not true. Could Donna Zalewski have made it up? Or imagined it?"

Rita looked down at Kimi, who was, for once, asleep, curled up under the table.

"Okay," I said. "You can't talk about Donna Zalewski. But don't you feel some responsibility about her? This is going to sound mean, but you are the one who sent her to Joel Baker. Maybe your professional responsibility is to do something now, not just to keep totally quiet about whatever she told you."

"Maybe," Rita said.

"Well, think about it." Then I pulled something on Rita that I learned from her. "Maybe you're not ready yet," I said, "but in the meantime, just talk to me a little about someone like her. Not about Donna Zalewski. Just about that kind of person. Okay? For instance, it seems to me that there are some women who could not be seduced by a therapist no matter what. Like Elaine Walsh, for example. Or, I don't know, maybe she's a bad example. Anyway, there are some women like that. And then there are others, I bet, who could be."

"There have been cases of women being told it was part of the therapy, that it was necessary for their benefit."

"Okay. And, obviously, not everybody is going to believe something like that. You're not. I'm not."

"And sometimes, the countertransference becomes so powerful that the therapist is overwhelmed. He isn't a sociopath. He doesn't mean to be exploitative. Sometimes, apparently, these people genuinely believe that they're in love with the women. In a way, of course, they are. But it doesn't justify it. It doesn't even begin to justify it."

"What's countertransference?"

"It's, um, it's a little complicated."

"So are the American Kennel Club obedience regulations."

"That's a rather different order of complexity." She coughed. "It has to do with the therapist's response to the client. What the therapist projects. How the therapist distorts the relationship."

"That doesn't make any sense," I objected. "Why would anybody go to a therapist who was going to do that? I mean, the point is sanity, right?"

"Sometimes the main point is another human being," Rita said. "And every human being has a past, a history. And anyone who's got a history has something to transfer to the new relationship. Anyway, it may be inevitable. But acting on it isn't."

"But look. Suppose the guy, the therapist, starts telling one of his woman patients—"

Rita interrupted. "Clients."

"Clients. So suppose he starts telling her that he's madly in love with her. I mean, if that happened, a lot of women would realize that there was something wrong with the therapist. If you saw a therapist who started telling you he was crazy about you, what would you do?"

"Go to a consultant. Instantly," she said, and added, "Another therapist. Somebody outside the situation, to put some perspective on what was going on and what to do about it."

"Even if you didn't know to do that, if you were someone who didn't know much about therapy, you'd still know something was really off, that that wasn't how therapy was supposed to be. And the reverse must be true. That there are women who wouldn't get it. Either they just didn't know much about therapy and didn't realize how taboo it is, or else they fell in love, too, or got caught up in believing it was for their own good."

"Yes."

"So was Donna Zalewski the kind of person who'd know? Who'd get it? Would she have told somebody to go to hell and walked out? Or was she vulnerable?"

"I'd have thought she'd have come back to me," Rita said.

"She didn't. But was she vulnerable?"

"There are people whose boundaries about everything are very diffuse." Rita had both elbows on the table. She folded her hands and rested her chin on them. "For people like that, relationships are never clearly defined. You can see it in every aspect of their lives. No one is separate from everyone else. Sometimes you find families where the kids can all go into the parents' bedroom unannounced whenever they feel like it. There's no lock on the bathroom door. And in a similar way, in terms of individuals, the doors and the locks, the walls, the boundaries, aren't there, either. You see, I've always thought that was one of Joel's strengths as a therapist, the ability to keep the boundaries very clear, which is one thing that makes people feel safe."

"This may sound stupid to you, but in a way, that's what Elaine didn't do with Kimi."

"This is serious," Rita said.

"It's true. There was no boundary between who was the owner and who was the dog. The first time I was there, she put a pitcher of milk on the table and just stood there and watched Kimi drink it. And that kind of thing makes a dog very nervous. They want to know who's who and what the rules are. They want to know where they belong in the pack and what they can and can't do. That's when they're happy. Otherwise, it's a crazy world for them, and they spend all their time trying to bring some order into it."

"I didn't refer her to Elaine Walsh," Rita said. "There are a lot worse clinicians than Elaine, but she had a tendency to let theory override her judgment."

"Like the marriage-is-slavery theory. So the Mosses' marriage didn't exist. The boundary didn't exist. The limits didn't. But that made it as if Sheila Moss didn't exist. Or as if her feelings didn't, or didn't count. I'm not sure which. But look. Elaine was obviously furious about Joel Baker. That taboo was one rule she recognized. She was going to turn him in."

"His life would have been ruined. And there wasn't really anything he could have done about it."

"Say he didn't do it?"

"And just how was he supposed to prove that? It would have been strictly Donna's word against his. That's a way in which therapists are very vulnerable."

"And Donna Zalewski?"

"If everything is diffuse, the boundary between what's real and what isn't can get very vague, too."

"She was very vulnerable."

"In a way, so was Elaine. She was vulnerable to believing it."

A while later, when Rita stood up and got ready to leave, Kimi clambered out from under the table, shook herself off, and stuck her big, black, wet nose directly in the crotch of Rita's navy wool pants.

"No!" I said firmly, and dragged her away. The worst thing about that habit is that public correction embarrasses the sniffed person even more than the dog already has. The best way to eradicate any unwelcome behavior isn't negative, anyway, but positive: Teach the dog what he *is* supposed to do. Lie down. Sit. Give his paw. Whatever. Once Kimi mastered heeling, sitting, and staying, she'd stop embarrassing herself, me, and other people. I'd get her there. In the meantime, I apologized.

But Rita has a dog, too. She smiled and shook her head. "I'm having awful cramps. Dogs can always tell."

"Yes," I said. "But they don't have to announce it to everyone else."

"Boundaries," Rita said.

Chapter 12

THERE are two notable institutions of higher learning in my neighborhood. The first is the Cambridge Dog Training Club. The second is a certain person-training club principally famous for the big bang produced by dropping its name.

In Cambridge, though, the high concentration of alumni and alumnae muffles the bang to what would sound like a thud if you didn't know better, but everyone does know better because there's always a Harvard graduate around to spell out the significance of everything to the rest of us. One of the lessons Harvard teaches the undergraduates is to question every assumption since Christ's. It's a lesson the graduates remember. For instance, the alumni don't assume that everyone knows they're alumni, and, despite their numbers, they don't assume that everyone in Cambridge went to Harvard any more than the owner of a purebred dog from great lines and a famous kennel assumes that your dog of the same breed is of equal rank. If you admit that you went someplace with a name that doesn't drop quite so loudly, the typical alumnus slowly lowers his eyes, silently expresses pity for you, and stops assuming that you know what he knows and have read what he's read. In fact, he may start assuming that you know nothing and can't read.

But I'm used to it. Dog people ask what kennel your dog came from, too, and sometimes they're more than simply curious. In truth, what dog snobs share with Ivy snobs is a mistrust of their own judgment. Some dog people need to ask where the dog came from because they don't trust themselves to recognize a good dog when they see one. The Ivy snobs don't trust themselves to recognize a smart person. Have I digressed?

I was still wondering what kind of person Donna Zalewski

had been, but my first guess about where she'd gone to college turned out to be right, and after some tedious time spent with the Harvard Alumni Directory, I placed two calls to Adams House and managed to get the name of her roommate, whose phone number I got from another look at the Harvard stud book. And what did I tell you? The ex-roommate lived in a graduate-student kennel on Wendell Street, which is a ten-minute walk from Harvard Yard. Cambridge is a great whelping box filled with litter after litter of full-grown, unweaned dogs. A sensible bitch would nip and growl at these people until they learned to feed themselves.

I told the former roommate, Sarah Goldberg, that I now owned Donna Zalewski's malamute, was having some problems with the dog, and thought it might help if I understood a little bit about both Donna and Kimi. I knew the story was farfetched, but as soon I mentioned the dog, Sarah seemed almost oddly willing to talk to me. She set up a time for us to meet and invited me to Wendell Street.

I've seen less crowded and better furnished whelping boxes than the railroad apartment that Sarah Goldberg shared with four or five other graduate students. The furniture must have come from Morgan Memorial and the Bargain Spot, but there was lots of it, overstuffed armchairs upholstered in scratchy blue-green and stained a pale mud color, sagging bookshelves with chipped paint, rickety wooden chairs, gouged tables, and, underneath, carpet remnants pieced together. But it wasn't depressing. It was like a happy, underfunded child-care center, a child-care center for semi-grown-ups. That's what graduate students are, of course: adult children. Adult children of academics.

Sarah was a tall, thin woman in her mid-twenties with long blond hair fastened in a ponytail at the base of her neck. She had a plain, bony, stark face and wore clothes that she must have picked up when she bought the furniture. The second we walked in, she made a heartfelt fuss over Kimi. I liked her right away. Kimi did, too, but then malamutes like almost anyone, especially anyone who'll play with them and pay attention to them.

Sarah finally looked at me. "God, she's wonderful. I want a dog so badly, but it's not fair to keep one here. We're gone all the time, and we're all broke. That's half the reason I can hardly wait to finish my dissertation."

"What kind of dog are you going to get?" I asked when we seated ourselves in the kitchen. We faced each other across a table. Maybe the benches we sat on were small church pews, or maybe the ensemble was a booth salvaged from a defunct restaurant.

"Oh, one of these. A malamute." She looked intelligent, too. "I've always loved malamutes. When I was growing up, some people down the block had one that was practically half mine. His name was Nicky. I used to walk him for them, fool around with him. He was my bosom companion. We grew up together."

"That's so strange," I said. "That you and Donna both . . ."

"Did Donna tell you . . . ?"

"I never met Donna." I shook my head. "I didn't know her at all."

"Then how . . . ?"

"The breeder she got Kimi from. She told the breeder about how she'd grown up with a malamute. That was one reason she wanted one."

Sarah pursed her lips and tilted her head a little as if she were hearing something familiar. "You didn't know Donna," she said.

"No."

"She did things like that sometimes."

I must have looked puzzled.

"She had a way of co-opting other people's experience. Sometimes it seemed fairly benign. Other times she'd give you the feeling that she was stealing your life."

"She didn't . . . ?"

Sarah sounded gentle. "She didn't grow up with a malamute down the block. I did." She shrugged. Then she suddenly smiled. "You must be wondering which of us borrowed the other's neighborhood dog."

I laughed. Nervously. "I'm just a little thrown." I made noises to attract Kimi's attention and get her to come to me, but she kept staring up at Sarah.

"I guess the easiest way to explain it is that Donna was a person who felt empty," Sarah said. "And when she was feeling particularly empty, she filled herself up. She took bits and pieces of other people's experience. She swallowed parts of people's lives like tranquilizers. Or antidepressants. In a way, it was flattering when she chose one's own life. But sometimes it was hard to look at it that way. Donna didn't have a lot of friends."

"You were roommates." I tried to keep my tone neutral, but Sarah understood.

"Question," she said. "Why would anyone room with Donna? Answer: She came with the suite. My freshman roommate and I moved into a suite in Adams House, and Donna was there. She was a senior. There were three bedrooms. She already had one of them. And at first, we thought she was so incredibly sophisticated." She smiled nostalgically. "She was from New York. She wore black clothes. Eye makeup. She read Kierkegaard. We were terribly impressed. She took organic chemistry because she needed a gut course that year. And that part was true. She was very bright. She took math and chemistry courses when she didn't want any work. She'd just take them and get A's, no matter how depressed she was. No matter how much of a mess. She'd be so nervous, her hands would be trembling, and she'd still get A's. That was true."

"And?"

"And the sophistication was what passes for sophistication in the eyes of two sophomores from little towns in the Midwest. And even then, we caught on pretty fast, and, once we did, she scared the shit out of us. She'd get on crying jags. Her hands would shake. And she'd get herself involved in these big, dramatic romances. Everyone was always trying to seduce her. Part of that was probably true. She was sort of naturally attractive. And when she was up, she was very up."

"And when she wasn't?"

"It sounds like the children's poem. When she was up, she was very, very up, and when she was down, she was frantic." Sarah made a wry face. "But it was distinctly unfunny."

"Was she in therapy?"

"She was seeing someone at the University Health Service. Anne Marie and I went to his office once. That was my roommate, Anne Marie. The whole situation was tougher for Anne Marie than it was for me, for some reason, and she talked to some people at Adams House, and we ended up talking to the psychiatrist. Mostly, he acted almost pathetically glad that

Donna had any friends at all. And really, we weren't. But partway through the year, Donna started getting a little better, and it got easier for us because we knew she was graduating, that it was only for a few months, and so forth."

"But you stayed in touch with her?"

"Not really. It was just that we were both in Cambridge, and we'd run into each other, which was how I knew she had a malamute. We had lunch together once. She was not my favorite person, but I suppose I was curious about her. Also, I always felt guilty. After listening to her psychiatrist? If Anne Marie and I were as close as she came to having friends . . ."

"How was she doing? If she was so . . . ?"

"At first, I thought she was doing better. She was even talking about getting a job."

"She didn't work?"

"She had an independent income. That was where I learned the phrase. I never even knew such a thing existed. It was like a title—marchioness, viscount. In theory, I knew there were people who had them, but in practice? Not people I knew. The money was part of Donna's problem, I think. If she'd ever actually had to support herself, or if she'd known that someday she'd have to, she might have had to pull herself together. And the time we had lunch, I thought at first she was finally going to do it. But then she started in on some of the old stuff."

"Like?"

"Another one of the seduction stories. Actually, it wasn't seduction. And it wasn't violent rape. It was forced intercourse. This time it was a therapist."

"Why are you so sure it was a story?"

"Mainly, I guess, because I'd heard it before. The characters varied, but the scene remained constant. One time it was a fine-arts professor. Another time it was somebody in the chemistry department."

"Did she ever make any of this public? Besides telling you? Go to someone in the university?"

"How could she?" Sarah raised her eyebrows. "It was all imaginary. Or most of it was."

By now, Kimi was half sitting in Sarah's lap.

"Could she have been, uh, misinterpreting things?" I asked. "I mean, if she was alone with someone in his office and he did something like shake her hand when she left . . . ?"

"Who knows? Maybe that's the kind of thing that triggered it. But that's not what her story was. Believe me. I had to hear all the details. Shaking hands did not play a prominent role. Intercourse did. Anyway, after she launched into the latest, with all the graphic details, I realized that some things had changed, and others hadn't."

"What was it that had changed? That she was talking about a job?"

"That was one thing. Another was . . . This is pretty repulsive. Are you sure you want to hear it?"

"No," I said. "But tell me, anyway."

"One of Donna's symptoms was, uh, a compulsion, I suppose, to sort of pick at herself."

"Criticize herself?"

"That was its abstract form. She did do that. But she also did it physically. She'd pick at her nails until the cuticles were all torn and bleeding, and she picked at her skin. She pulled hair." She made a pinching gesture with the thumb and index finger of her right hand.

I reached a hand up to my hair.

"Sometimes," Sarah said. "But it wasn't so much that. In a way, it was worse. Mostly, she'd pull out the hair on her arms. The skin would be red and irritated-looking. She'd keep rubbing the area. It was disgusting. I warned you, didn't I? But the day we had lunch, last summer, she had on a dress with short sleeves, and I could see she hadn't been doing it. So I thought she was doing better. Donna was a very sick person. I know that's not a popular word, but it's true. I wasn't surprised when I heard."

Chapter 13

"Talk to me," I said to Kimi. "Tell me all about it." We were heeling down Appleton Street toward Huron Avenue. Her leash was in my left hand, and I was using my voice to keep her attention. Mostly my voice. Marissa believed in appealing to a dog's finer instincts and desire to please. She trained golden retrievers. Malamutes want to please, too. Themselves. And they have fine instincts—fine for survival in the Arctic. One of Rowdy's finest, I'd learned, was his appetite, and it was one of Kimi's, too. If, as Buck believes, Marissa and all of her goldens look down upon us from heaven, I hoped that she either couldn't see or could forgive the dried liver in the pockets of my parka and in both of my gloves. But I was using my voice, too.

"Good girl. Nice work. Heel. Good. Super! Let's go! Nice. It didn't hurt, did it? I don't think it did. If it had, you would have taken a nice, good big chunk out of her, wouldn't you? That's my lovely Kimi. Sit." I pulled gently on the leash and guided her into a straight sit at my side, so she wouldn't discover the wrong way. "Good girl. Kimi, heel! She just rubbed and plucked gently, didn't she? She didn't want to hurt you, did she? She just couldn't help it. Kimi, heel! Easy does it. Good work."

Down the block. Back home. With a beginner like Kimi, it's important to keep training sessions lively and brief. Besides, it was four below zero that day, and I had two dogs to groom. We were going to a show. Kimi, of course, wasn't ready to enter in a children's pet parade. I hadn't registered Rowdy for the show, either, because he already had his C.D. and wasn't yet ready for Open, which is the class you enter when you're going for a C.D.X., the next title, Companion Dog Excellent. I could have put him in Graduate Novice, which is between Novice and Open—no title, just experience and ribbons—but the show we were going to had only the regular obedience trial classes, no Graduate Novice. So why the grooming? It isn't even mandatory for obedience, but there's always that chance that Buck is right. Marissa might forgive liver in the pockets, but if she saw me walk into a show with two unbathed dogs, she'd materialize and grab them both away from me.

When malamutes are shedding, removing brushful after brushful of the soft, woolly undercoat is exactly like shearing a flock of sheep, and the only sane place to do it is outdoors, but since neither Kimi nor Rowdy was shedding, we used the kitchen floor. The only problem I had was that they both wanted to lie on their backs and have their tummies stroked with the soft natural-bristle brush and didn't want to stand up and let me do the rest of them. I did them together because, of course, I wanted to compare their responses. Did Kimi shy away? Did something bother her that didn't bother Rowdy? Not a thing. It seemed to me that she had been used badly, but not, from her point of view, abused.

I am stronger than I look. I forced Rowdy into the tub and kept him there until he was clean. I didn't get bitten. I did get wet. While he started to drip dry, I drained and refilled the tub for Kimi. I wasn't sure I had any strength left for the second battle, but it was obvious that she'd been taught—and not by Elaine Walsh—not only to get into a tub but even to enjoy it a little.

"Either Donna taught you this herself," I told Kimi as I sprayed water through her coat, "or she had you groomed by somebody who was nice to you. But I think she did it herself." Professional groomers generally don't share their own bathtubs with their clients because it would be too hard on their backs. They use raised tubs, and the dogs don't climb in the way Kimi had climbed into my bathtub. "I think she tried to be good to you," I said. "She got you from Faith. She took you to Steve. She kept you clean. She didn't really hurt you. She loved you. She was just very sick."

"She stopped picking at herself," I told Rita. "And she started on Kimi instead."

The world's most beautiful Alaskan malamutes were bouncing around and showing off for her. I was a mess. I'd scrubbed out the bathtub, but the Liquid-plumr had to sit in the drain for twenty more minutes before I'd be able to take a shower myself. Steel wool in the drain opening catches most of the fur, but not all.

"Would Kimi have put up with that?" Rita asked. "Would any dog?"

"Plucking is a normal part of grooming some breeds," I said. "Besides, I'm really sure she didn't hurt Kimi. When Sarah first told me about it, about Donna, and I realized what she'd done, I was furious, but then I realized that this is not an abused dog. She just is not. If she'd been hurt, she'd show some sign, and she doesn't. Handle her, pat her, groom her, and she's no different from Rowdy. She's a lot easier to bathe. You know what it reminds me of? You know how little kids will rub the fur off their stuffed animals?"

"That's a benign interpretation," Rita said.

"I think maybe it was like that. It's still sick, though. But, look, is the other part possible? That she quit picking at herself and started on Kimi instead? Just in theory. Do people do that?"

"Displace it? It's possible. I've never heard of it. Here's what I can tell you. Maybe it'll help. A symptom like that never means just one thing, and it never serves just one function. Also, Freud said that every symptom is a compromise. It's the best compromise a person can reach. Does that make sense to you?"

"That maybe it was both? Is that what you're saying? What she did to Kimi was picking at herself and also the stuffed-animal thing?"

"Maybe. The truth is, I'm more concerned about Joel Baker. I was the one who referred her to Joel in the first place. I keep thinking that I'm the one who put him in jeopardy. I wonder how many people have heard that story."

"Sarah says that Donna didn't have a lot of friends. You can see why. So she probably didn't have a lot of people to tell. And you never really believed it. Did you?"

"Oh, I wondered. I'd like to think I didn't believe it, that I dismissed it. But I did wonder. You know, it's like some virulent infection, a rumor like that. Once you've caught it, it doesn't just go away. Once you hear that a therapist has been sleeping with his clients, or with one of them, it infects your thinking. I still feel doubt."

"Do you really think he . . . ?"

"No. I've mulled it over a lot, and I think he probably didn't. I know him. And even statistically, it's unlikely. He's a psychologist. I mean, that's why our malpractice insurance is so cheap. Mine is something like three hundred and fifty dollars a year, and for psychiatrists, it's a lot more than that. Psychologists don't get sued, not very often, not the way M.D.'s do. But even so, I feel doubt. I feel mistrust. And all it takes is enough people like me who hesitate, and he stops getting referrals, and that's it."

"You know what I don't understand? Why did Elaine believe her?"

"How was Elaine supposed to know? Therapists don't go out and cross-question all of their clients' friends. We work for clients, not their friends."

"So how do you ever know the truth about them? All you get are their versions."

"That's the truth we're after. We aren't outside investigators trying to find some objective reality."

"But what if the person's reality is totally off base?"

"By whose standards?"

"Anybody's."

"By a lot of people's standards, your reality is a little off base. Dogs are not all that prominent a feature of most people's reality."

"Precisely," I said.

"Which is precisely why you go to dog training instead of therapy, because this dog obsession isn't a problem for you. It's a successful adaptation. It's satisfying for you. You have fun with it. People come to therapy when their adaptive efforts don't work, when adaptive efforts go badly astray. Or backfire. Or when they're hopelessly at variance with other people's realities in a way that gets them in trouble."

"I would have thought . . ."

"Dogs don't cure everything."

"Well, she did stop picking at herself," I said. "If Kimi had known that, in a way, she was helping Donna feel better, she probably wouldn't have minded, especially if she'd known that

Donna was that desperate. But I still can't see how she could have done that to Kimi. There's something so disgusting about it."

Rita shrugged.

"Do you think Elaine knew?" I asked.

"I don't know."

"And how could she not know that Donna was lying about Joel? And why would Donna have lied to her, anyway? I mean, what's the point? Why would anybody go to a therapist and then lie? And you know what else? Why would Donna have picked Joel Baker of all people? He's a perfectly nice guy. And before, she never really did anything. Really, what she did was put on a show for her roommates. Maybe that's all she wanted to do with Elaine."

"I wouldn't be too hard on Elaine about it," Rita said. "Partly, she was responding to the climate of the times. The truth is that women do get abused, and until recently, lots of women had no recourse. There was nothing they could do about it. They had to keep it private. And furthermore, they received every encouragement to blame themselves for it."

"So Elaine thought Donna was one more woman like that."

"Elaine believed in going public. She believed in assertiveness. Action. And, you know, it's remotely possible that she had reason. It's possible that Joel was somehow . . . It does happen."

"You know what's so terrible? In a way, it wouldn't have mattered. If Elaine had gone to that board and reported him, and if the whole thing had ended up in the papers, how many people would have bothered to find out what really happened? How could anybody know for sure? All of these people would have said what you just said: that it was possible. He could be a saint, and people could shrug and say, 'Oh, well, it's possible.' No matter what, there was no way he could have defended himself. That bothers me—that he couldn't have defended himself."

"That's a problem," Rita said.

"I guess he did find some way, after all," I said. "But it doesn't seem fair that murder should have been his only option."

Chapter 14

FOR dependable personal protection, I trust the brand more women ought to prefer—the Alaskan malamute—but on the morning of the show, the protection I needed wasn't from muggers and rapists. I washed down two tablets of Advil with a cup of coffee.

The show site was the Northeast Trade Center in Woburn, just off the highway that everyone in Massachusetts calls Route 128 even though it's been 95 and not just 128 for years. On the same principle, the premium lists and entry blanks for the shows at the Northeast Trade Center always call it a beautiful show site. When 95 was nothing but 128, maybe it was. But all show sites really are beautiful, in more ways than one. First of all, places that are large enough for a dog show and also willing to put up with one are so rare that having a site at all is beautiful. That's why practically all premium lists tell you to behave yourself so the club can use the beautiful site again. If the exhibitors let their dogs soil all over the show grounds, the club sponsoring the show will have to find another place to rent for next year's.

Mostly, though, any site is a beautiful sight once the dogs arrive. For an aesthetic experience, forget museums. For beauty, you need animation, life, motion, change, feeling, excitement, suspense, diversity, contrast, meaning, and love, not to mention unity, proportion, order, and harmony. Marble and bronze are cold, and you probably won't be allowed to touch them, anyway. Paintings are static, and they won't lick your face. Besides, at a museum, you already know who won. What is beauty? Order. Sporting group, nonsporting group, working group, herding group, hounds, terriers, and toys. Proportion?

Rest your eyes on the Best in Show. Balance? Both breed and obedience. Contrast? Oh, yes. In size, shape, color, and national origin. Irish wolfhounds. Skye terriers. Spinoni italiani. Collies. Unity? Unity is best of all. Kuvasok, Dobermans, Irish water spaniels, Basenjis, Cavalier King Charles spaniels, Akitas, Maltese, Belgian Malinois, Dalmatians, Tibetan terriers . . . Giant, toy, noisy, silent, hairless, furry, they're all dogs. The next time the world starts looking ugly, don't search for beauty in some static tomb. Go to the greatest multimedia, multisensory art exhibit in the world. Go to a dog show.

Kimi, for example, found the beauty almost overwhelming, and although it wasn't Rowdy's first show, his aesthetic sense was so refined that show after show had left him as unjaded as the first. That's why we were there, of course, to transform my aesthetes into pragmatists. Take them to enough shows, and they'll learn to ignore the beauty that bombards them and start concentrating on the practical business of getting good scores in obedience.

Beauty was manifesting itself in the form of a well-stocked booth displaying the wares of the IAMS pet food company, manufacturers of IAMS cat food, dog biscuits, and a variety of dog foods. Kimi was sniffing one of the big bags of Eukanuba that sat on the floor in front of the booth, but Rowdy, the sophisticate, had set his sights high, namely, on the pile of free samples arrayed on the table at malamute nose level. I'd just finished a long and interesting discussion about ethoxyquin with the IAMS representative (and collected a pamphlet on the subject of that highly debated preservative as well as two sample bags of low-calorie dog food) when I spotted Joel and Kelly Baker collecting free samples at the neighboring Science Diet booth.

Kelly was wearing a hand-knit Irish sweater like one I'd admired in the L. L. Bean catalog, but decided not to order because it was too expensive. Instead, I got an encyclopedia of rare breeds, two obedience books, a text on canine genetics, a grooming guide, a gallon of dog shampoo, and a Nylafloss dental device—a ham-scented dental-floss bone for dogs—from a mail-order discount pet supply house, and I had some money left over, too. Until I saw Kelly in the sweater, I didn't regret the decision.

"Hi, there," I said. "How'd you do?"

It was a safe question. Joel and Kelly had that relaxed, smug look of people whose dogs have done well. By the way, if—God forbid—you've never been to a dog show, you may imagine that I had to shout to make myself heard over the yapping of thousands of dogs. Actually, every dog show generates a tremendous amount of yapping, but it's nearly all human. The loudspeakers kept blaring out announcements, the people kept prattling, and most of the dogs were silent.

"Tuck went BOS," Kelly said. That stands for Best of Opposite Sex. If Best of Breed goes to a dog, Best of Opposite goes to a bitch, and vice versa.

"Congratulations. That's great," I said to both of them, then added, to Joel, "You handle her yourself, don't you?"

He nodded. He was dressed for the breed ring—a good wool suit in a Ridgeback shade of tan, an off-white shirt, and a brown tie—but unlike most dog people, he usually dressed that way, except, of course, that his clothes didn't always color-coordinate with the dogs. His blond hair looked newly trimmed, and I'd never seen him when he wasn't closely shaved. Nowhere in the American Kennel Club regulations does it stipulate that handlers have to dress up, but they all do, at least in breed. In obedience, those of us who respect the sport always dress presentably, but certain other people not raised by my mother look like slobs.

"Good for you. I hate to see it go all professional," I said. "Even though I do it myself. I show Rowdy in obedience myself, but I have a handler for breed. But we aren't entered today. We're just here for the experience. We snuck in."

Both of my dogs had been harmlessly comparing the new scent of Science Diet to the familiar one of Eukanuba, but Kimi was starting to paw at a twenty-pound bag, and I didn't want to fund a taste test.

"Rowdy, heel," I said. He came smoothly to my left side and sat squarely. "Kimi, leave it." I took a couple of steps and hauled her as gently as I could away from the bag of dog food. You're allowed to warm your dog up before you enter the obedience ring, but otherwise, training is strictly forbidden on show grounds.

"You going to do an obedience brace?" Joel asked. "Or breed? They look marvelous, don't they?"

I loved the man, of course.

"Thanks," I said. "I don't know about Kimi yet. I haven't had her long. I'm just starting to work with her."

"She's a sweetie," said Kelly, who was chucking Kimi under the chin, massaging the thick fur around her neck, and making soft noises to her. Kelly's shiny, curly dark hair echoed Kimi's glossy dark wolf gray, and Kelly's white sweater picked up Kimi's white trim.

Joel reached into his pocket and gestured to me with his closed fist. "All right?"

Carrying food into the obedience ring is prohibited, but, in breed, all handlers use food to bait the dogs. If you're a newcomer to dog shows and you've been wondering why the dogs all look so alert in the breed ring, that's the answer to your question: liver.

"Sure," I said. *No. I'm pretty sure you murdered two women, and I don't trust you with my dogs.* Obviously, I did trust him. With dogs.

He smacked his lips, held his closed fist near Kimi's nose to attract her attention, and then lifted his fist up and held his other arm out. She took the bait, rising on her powerful hindquarters and resting her forepaws on Joel's outstretched arm. Her muscles rippled, and her eyes gleamed. Even if you've spent your entire life around beautiful dogs, there are moments when you see dogs as if for the first time. She looked spectacular. Joel opened his fist and fed her the liver.

"See what fun shows are?" I said to her.

Rowdy was still sitting at heel and, as he'd been taught, not leaning on me, but I could still feel him quiver. I looked down. A stream of drool was pathetically cascading from his mouth.

"Did we forget you?" I asked him.

"Of course not," Kelly said, reaching into her pocket and then offering him his share of the treat. "This is a beautiful dog. Aren't you? And are you a good boy? You sure are." She reached back into her pocket.

"That's probably enough," I said. "They don't do too well around food yet. I have to feed them separately."

Rowdy understood the tone of my voice—and maybe, just maybe, my words—and looked up at me in the hope that I'd change my mind, but Kimi was still sniffing around. She checked out Kelly's hands, licked them, and conducted a careful survey of the floor beneath Rowdy's mouth in case he'd dropped any liver. He hadn't. She raised her pretty head and discovered a fascinating new scent. We'd been at the show for a couple of hours, and, as Rita had said, dogs always know. Kimi's nostrils twitched, and her face took on that bright, transported expression that always reminds me of the picture in the children's book that shows Ferdinand the bull smelling the flowers. No. *Red Flower,* I thought. It was a book Elaine Walsh had tried to get me to read. An entire book about menstruation. Is that incredible? I told Elaine that as soon as I'd gone through all of the three or four thousand dog books written in English, everything ever published about the Celtics, and then every book that had a plot, I'd give it a try.

I obviously hadn't mastered the dog books I'd already read, because I wasn't quick enough. Kimi pressed her nose against my crotch. Elaine would probably have lectured me on the foolishness of my embarrassment. But Elaine was dead.

"Shoo," I said quietly, pulling at her leash, and Kelly tried to rescue me.

"Kimi!" Kelly knew how to animate her voice. At the sound of her own name, Kimi turned to Kelly, but something distracted her. A different scent.

No. Not quite. She pointed her head back toward me, sniffed, then just as if speaking aloud in the high, clear tones of a precocious child, darted toward Joel and pressed her nose against his crotch. "Oh! You, too!" she announced. I gave a sharper pull on her leash than the American Kennel Club would have liked to see on the grounds of a show.

"Well, congratulations on Tuck." My voice sounded false. "We'd better be going. Nice to see you."

Well, what was I supposed to say? Was I supposed to say what was on my mind? How could I? If Kimi had spoken English, she couldn't have told me more clearly and explicitly that Joel, too, was having his period. You don't believe me? A human being has about five million olfactory cells. A dog has two hundred million, and those canine cells are more sensitive than ours. Furthermore, dogs process information about odor better than we do because the part of a dog's brain that deals with scent is better developed than ours. All in all, a dog's nose is about a million times better than a person's. On top of that— in spite of what Rita is always saying about wishes—when my dogs communicate their observations to me, I understand what

I'm being told. You still don't trust me? Don't. It doesn't matter. Once Kimi said it, everything else about Joel fell into place: His prettiness. His build. His clothes—suits, ties, topcoats, male shoes, nothing a woman would wear, nothing unisex. In fact, he had to dress like a man because that's what he wasn't.

Rita says that this anomalous observation precipitated a brief and benign state of dissociation. "So he's having his period," I remember saying to myself. "I'm having mine, too." The next thing I remember is stopping at a concession booth where I bought a bright red coupler to connect the dogs' collars so I could walk them on one leash and—someday—show them as an obedience brace. It was a sensible enough, if optimistic, purchase. I also bought a bottle of Burnished Bronze dog shampoo, presumably for use on my nonbronze dogs, a large container of Ever Clean cat litter, a book on dog tricks that I already had at home, and a T-shirt that read: "Love Is a Great Dane." I have never owned a Great Dane. At another stand, I bought a pound of raisin and nut trail mix, exactly the kind I hate most. Finally, I bought a hideous plate with a hand-painted picture of a Labrador retriever holding a dead bird in its mouth. Did I intend all of these things for someone else? Don't ask me.

Eventually, of course, the dogs brought me to my senses. Returning people to normal is a canine specialty. Rowdy started woo-wooing, and Kimi joined in. When Alaskan malamutes woo-woo like that, it's obvious that they are not merely venting their feelings. No, they are insistently addressing *you*, and you'd better listen. I did.

Chapter 15

I broke the news to Rita the next day. She was, if anything, even less eager to believe it than I'd been. In fact, she didn't believe me. "Dogs sniff," she said. "They sniff everyone."

"I do speak dog, you know," I said. "It happens to be my native language. I'm perfectly fluent. If you knew I'd grown up in Budapest and I told you what somebody said in Hungarian, would you tell me I'd misunderstood?"

We were eating lunch at Pentimento, which is on Huron Avenue, only a few blocks from my house, and will be terrific once the management stops groveling to the so-called health inspectors. Health! If the government is really serious about keeping restaurants free from a species that spreads disease, the inspectors ought to issue warnings and then close down any eatery that allows *Homo sapiens* on the premises. Do dogs carry influenza, TB, and strep? No. You can't even catch a cold from a dog. Steve agrees with me, of course, but he's too concerned about his practice to take action. He worries that human clients might not trust a radical veterinarian.

In the meantime, in spite of the dogless environment, Pentimento manages to serve a grand dessert—Denver chocolate pudding—a combination chocolate cake and pudding, and you can order it topped with about eight ounces of whipped cream.

Is it necessary to advertise Denver chocolate pudding to explain how Rita reacted to the news that Joel Baker was a woman? Perhaps you have the impression that I am digressing. Maybe you share Rita's conviction that a person who feels anxious about something blathers on about anything else instead. Maybe you are right. But the pudding is really good, anyway.

"You're probably going to have seconds, aren't you?" Rita

said. When she recently discovered that her one pair of jeans wouldn't zip, she started on a high-protein liquid diet, but declared today a solid-food holiday. I don't know why she cared. She's tiny, and she hardly ever wears jeans, anyway. Most of the time, she has on the kind of outfit she was wearing that day, an olive-green silk suit with an off-white sweater and chunky gold jewelry. I was wearing jeans and a wool sweater that were on the verge of demotion to kennel clothes.

"No. I won't be hungry for at least another hour," I said meanly. Rita insists that dogs have given me some kind of parasite that spares me high-protein liquid. "The problem is that you'd like to see a dividing line between therapists and clients, and what I'm telling you is the line isn't there. It's so strange that you just won't see it."

"Who was it who recently said that this dog obsession of yours represented a healthy adaptation? She ought to lose her license. Can I have a bite of that?"

"Finish it. Or I'll treat you to one."

"No. Please." She pushed the bowl back toward me, but dipped her spoon into the goo and worked her way through it while we talked.

"For one thing, he's very short. For a man."

"That means nothing," Rita said, and, lowering her voice, added, "Don't use names."

"I'm not. And by itself, it does mean nothing. Spud Webb is shorter than I am."

"Who's Spud Webb?"

"Never mind."

"Oh, no," she said. "A famous dog."

"No. Dogs are not my only interest."

"A basketball player."

"How did you guess? Anyway, it's unusual for a man to be that short, and not just for basketball players. Then look at his face. His features are small, too. And his body? The narrow shoulders?"

"Normal variation."

"His voice."

"Haven't you got over that yet?"

"But the main thing is the beard."

"He is very fair-skinned. He has very light blond hair. His ancestors were probably Swedish or something. Nobody with that coloring has a five o'clock shadow. Besides, I'm sure I would've noticed if he had none. If he had a perfectly smooth face."

"Well, I've noticed," I said. "What I've noticed is that he always looks as if he's just finished shaving, and you know what? I'm sure he does shave. Lots of women have a little hair on their faces. If it bothers them, they go and have it waxed, right? How come? So they don't end up looking and feeling as if they have whiskers. That's why they don't shave it. Because they'd look like bearded ladies. You'd be able to feel the stubble. And see it. And that is what we're both seeing on him, what everybody's seeing. That's how it's done. I've thought this all out. Would you just consider the possibility?"

"I've known him for years. I've known them both for years. Among other things, they're two of the most conventional people I know. Their marriage is so traditional that, in Cambridge at least, they practically stand out."

"Oh, sorry. Then I must be wrong."

"It has happened before," Rita said. "There are some famous cases. Like, who was it who died just a while ago? Some musician, somebody fairly famous who lived as a man, but then turned out to be a woman. It was in all the papers. And, in fact, there's a new book about the whole phenomenon. I read a review somewhere. And you know what? I didn't buy the book. How come? Because I didn't want to read about it. You know what else? I don't want to hear about it. And you know why that is? Because it's too damned bizarre."

"Rita, bizarre is your business."

"You got it. Do you have any idea how often I have to listen to things that nobody wants to hear? That is my business. Horrible, horrible things happen to people, and people need to be able to tell someone about them. And half of me is that someone. And the other half of me is just like everyone else. There are times when I want to say, 'Look. I can't handle this. It's too much. Stop telling me about it because I don't want to hear it.' Okay? You're not even my patient. I don't want to hear it."

"The point is," I said, "think of the bind he was in."

"He?"

"He."

Rita nodded. "Okay. He."

"Anyway, can you imagine? Suppose you-know-who goes to

this board the way her letter said, and he gets called up. Well, he's got the perfect defense. I mean, for most men, there's nothing they can do. It's just one person's word against another's, and these days, everybody is biased in favor of the woman. Only in this case, he can absolutely prove that she's lying."

"But he pays a price." She sounded skeptical.

"That's the bind. You want to split another one of these Denver chocolate puddings?"

Rita groaned. "No. This whole thing is making me sick to my stomach."

"So either way, he loses everything, right? Either he's abused a client, or he's living this bizarre life, which isn't bizarre now, of course, not in the eyes of other people, because no one knows about it. But once it gets in the papers, he's either a criminal or a freak, in the public eye. And it's not just him. Can you imagine him letting that happen to her? One day, there she is, the greatest cook in the world, looking after the dogs, wanting a baby. For all I know, they'll end up adopting. And the next day, it's all over the front page of the *Globe* and the *Herald.*"

"Not to mention the *National Enquirer.*"

"I want him not to have done it," I said. "Before, I guess I had a . . . sort of a trace of doubt about him. That, you know, it was possible. That maybe he did do what she said. That she'd been crying wolf, and now it really happened. Or, this time, she made it happen. She seduced him. And first he tried to shut her up." I dropped my voice even though the restaurant was clearing out. "But Elaine kept on, anyway, on principle. She believed it was suicide, but that probably just made her more determined than ever to get him for it, because she must have thought the suicide was his fault. But now? God, he must have hated Elaine. You can hardly blame him. I can't imagine anything more unfair."

"Have you told Kevin about this, uh, new hypothesis?"

"I haven't seen him. Actually, I've been avoiding him. And if *you* think it's freakish and *you* think it's so bizarre that you're denying it . . ."

If there's one thing that enrages a therapist, it's being accused of denying something.

Rita interrupted. "I am not denying anything. Refusing to believe something totally improbable isn't denial. It's good reality-testing."

"You didn't see Kimi."

"Kimi. Who spoke to you."

"In her own language."

Rita studied the ceiling.

"You see?" I said. "If this is the response I get from you, how do you suppose Kevin would react? He probably wouldn't believe me, but if he did? Nonjudgmental openness to the extremes of human variation isn't exactly what you can expect from him."

"He's a Cambridge cop. And he grew up here. He's hardly lived a sheltered life. If something exists, it probably exists in Cambridge, and he's probably seen it. That's why he won't believe you, because even for Cambridge, this is too far beyond the pale. But you did show him those letters."

"Actually, I didn't. And I don't know if he's looked on the hard drive. Or maybe she had copies somewhere else, hard copy or something. Something the police would've found."

"So why haven't you . . . ?"

"The motive is so big," I said. "Especially now. Can you imagine Kevin's reaction, even before? And now? I'm right, you know, and he just might believe me. And once he did? Nobody would look for anything else. Nobody would even consider the possibility that he wasn't guilty."

"Do you?"

"Yes," I said. "So he had the strongest motive in the world. Maybe it ended there. Maybe somebody did him a favor."

"Who?"

"For one thing, somebody who had a lot of this drug, Sinequan. Somebody who didn't know she hated cottage cheese. He probably didn't know that, but where could he have got the stuff? And how would he have got it into the carton? Was there somebody else who could have? And who had some reason to, besides him? Rita, these people are living the most weird life. It's a weird way to live. But you know what's the weirdest thing? These are nice people. And you know what else? Not only are they likable, but I happen to like them. Rita, you know them. They are very nice people, and if I say anything to Kevin, they're not going to stand a chance. And absolutely everyone in Cambridge will know everything. Have you ever been to their house?"

"Yes."

"Well?"

"If you honestly think that he did these things, you can't keep it to yourself. It's not like this hypothesis you have about him. And, by the way, you aren't necessarily wrong."

"Thanks."

"Some of it does fit. I can see it. The truth is, I don't believe Kimi spoke to you, but once the possibility arises . . . anyway, the two issues are separate. Murdering people is not just one more alternative life-style. If he did this, I don't want him getting away with it. You didn't know Donna."

"I knew Elaine. And I liked her. I liked her a lot. And maybe now I don't like her quite as much I did then, but she meant what she said. And about that other stuff, I really don't think she meant to cause pain. She honestly did not believe in marriage. Literally. She would not recognize it. She did not mean to cause pain. And for all I know, maybe she didn't. I'm not at all sure that you-know-who knew about it."

"You-know-who with the Birkenstock sandals is married to an M.D.," Rita said. "Have you thought about that?"

"Not much, though she does do his billing. She told me that night I was there. Besides everything else, she was going to do their billing, she said. So if she sends his bills to his patients, she'd have known that Donna saw him, right? And she'd have Donna's address. And obviously she'd know where Elaine lived. Maybe she knew what he prescribed for Donna, even before."

"I don't see what she'd have against Donna, but that wasn't necessarily—"

"I don't either. Unless . . ."

"Unless what?"

"You're the one who said that psychiatrists pay a lot for malpractice because they get sued, and presumably they get sued because they're more apt to—"

"Holly, just because they pay a lot for their insurance, it doesn't mean they're all guilty of malpractice. Not at all. But about her? The billing? Maybe it does raise possibilities. But you're right about what Kevin would probably make of all this."

"I hope I'm wrong about Joel. If I decide I'm not, I'm going to have to tell Kevin."

"I hope you're wrong, too."

The waitress appeared. "Coffee?" she asked.

"Decaf," Rita said. "With cream?"

"Real," I said. "Caf."

The waitress left.

"I always think that decaf coffee is like safe sex," Rita said nostalgically.

Chapter 16

"A women's libber and a pill pusher," Kevin said. "Both. And proud of it."

We were discussing Dr. Ben Moss as we made our way around Fresh Pond at what I considered to be a running pace. Kevin wasn't even breathing hard. Rowdy, heeling nicely at Kevin's side but on leash, anyway, could have matched or beaten Kevin's normal speed, but his pink-red tongue was still hanging out. It does when he smiles. I had to keep passing Kimi's leash from one hand to the other as she bounced around me, tearing out in front, lagging behind, and levitating in joy.

"Rita says it's a fine art," I panted. "She says that some people can't function without medication and that picking the right stuff is a fine art. But she says Moss is no expert."

"Psycho," Kevin said, and then finished the word, stretching out the syllables, "pharmacology."

"Are you on some kind of holistic health kick?" Kimi suddenly stuck her nose in some leafless shrubbery and yanked me to an abrupt halt. "Kimi, let's go!"

"No." Kevin made a dismissive gesture with one of his beefy hands. "No. But the guy is an arrogant jerk."

"Could we slow down a little?"

"Sorry."

"It's okay. He was having an affair with Elaine Walsh. Rita told me."

"Yeah," Kevin said.

"You knew?"

"Yeah."

"How? Does he admit it?"

"Christ, *admit* it?" He shook his head back and forth.

"He bragged about it? Is that what's bothering you?"

Kevin has pale, almost translucent skin that freckles heavily in the summer, but since it was midwinter, his face turned an almost uniform red. The sky and its reflection in the pond were that bright winter gray that brings out the depth and highlights in his red hair. When he flushed, his whole head blazed.

"Was this some sort of locker room conversation?" I tried to catch my breath. "You thought he was being indecent?"

"First him. Now you."

"He told you that you were being prudish or something?"

"He tells me women are equal. Then he proceeds to tell me how. Graphically."

"You know, you really are a prude." I slowed down. "What did he say? That she was, uh, imaginative? Is that euphemistic enough? That she was unconventional?"

"Not in those words." He moved a little ahead of me.

"Well, that is offensive," I said. "She wouldn't have liked that. Or I don't think so. I don't think she thought kiss-and-tell was an essential part of liberation. Slow down, would you? And there is something indecent about it. I can see why you were offended. So why did he do it? Couldn't he see that he was making a bad impression? What was the point?"

"Oh, I got the point." Kevin was a couple of steps ahead of me. He turned his head so I could hear him clearly and added, "The point was, 'Why would a guy murder such a great lay?' "

"Kevin, Elaine would have overdosed you both if she'd heard that. Slow the hell down, would you? I'm not training for the marathon." Kevin was. He always is. "But what about the drug? The Sinequan?"

"Nothing there. Yes, he handed it out to Miss Zalewski. No, he didn't think she was a suicide risk. He has been forced to ask himself why he selected the drug. He has gone so far as to go to some other shrink to quote, work on the issue, unquote. With the assistance of the other shrink he has quote, recovered a memory, unquote."

"Of what?"

"It seems that a long time ago, the pharmaceutical company that pushes this stuff was trying to get doctors to prescribe it. So they didn't just advertise. They offered inducements."

"Like what?"

"They gave away records of classical music."

"You must be kidding."

"Fact. And Moss quote, recovered a memory, unquote of getting into the habit of prescribing Sinequan because he liked the free records. When he writes out a prescription for it, he hears violins playing in his head. And he likes the violins."

"So did he want a whole orchestra so badly that he gave Elaine some, too?"

"No. Not to Miss Walsh."

"Not 'Miss,' " I said. "Look, what is this macho need to set a pace that's just a little too fast for me? If you want to race, find someone your own size and give me Rowdy. I can handle them both."

"Sorry."

"I'm not a runner, you know. I only do this because the dogs need the exercise. So, did he prescribe it for anyone who knew Elaine? What did he say about that?"

"Squat," Kevin said.

"That it was none of your business? They have to do that. They can't go around talking about their clients. Patients. Whatever you call them. It really is confidential."

"No kidding. Do you need to stop?"

"No. You're in a great mood about this, aren't you?"

"The neighbors didn't notice a thing," Kevin said. "No suspicious characters had been hanging around Upland Road. No nuts had been threatening her. The only nut case we've got is a lady who thinks that all the dogs in Cambridge are conspiring against her, and since she got my name, she calls twenty times a day to tell me there's another one in her garden and will I send someone to arrest it."

"That woman on Lakeview," I said. "This is fine. You see? It's not that slow. The one with the strange garden, with the rocks that look like tombstones. Wait a minute, would you?"

Kimi lifted her leg on a section of the fence that runs between the path and the pond. Fresh Pond is a reservoir. No swimming. All bodies of fresh water in Massachusetts are reservoirs. Sometimes I get homesick for Maine. When Kimi finished, Rowdy covered her scent with his.

"Green, her name is," Kevin said, moving into a jog. "Rowdy, heel."

"Yes. How appropriate."

"Ms. Zalewski," he said pointedly, "lived on the same block. The woman is a total nut case from the word go."

"Don't let Rowdy forge like that," I said. "Is there some way this woman could've got hold of the Sinequan? I mean, if she really is that disturbed, maybe she had it prescribed for her. You know, I've gotten relaxed about Kimi. I mean, I went through that scare, worrying that someone was trying to poison her. Then, nothing's happened. There hasn't been a thing. So I've been pretty relaxed about it." In truth, of course, I'd quit worrying because I knew that Joel Baker wouldn't harm a dog, but I wasn't about to say that to Kevin. I wasn't about to mention Joel's name to him. "Could this woman have got hold of Sinequan? Did you check that out?"

"It never crossed my mind," he said. "You weren't around to tell me what to think."

"So you did check it out. Did she?"

"Not that we can tell." Then he repeated it. "Not that we can tell."

"Well, what do you think about her? You think it's possible? That she was after Kimi? Both times?"

"For what it's worth, in my opinion, she's a harmless nut. But if you see anyone hanging around, let me know."

"Of course. Hey, there's something I wanted to ask you. About the cottage cheese?"

"Yeah?"

"You found the carton, right?"

"Yeah."

"And you found the drug in it, right? There were traces of Sinequan in the carton?"

"Yeah."

"Okay. So it was mixed in, wasn't it? It wasn't just sprinkled on top. If it had just been on the top layer, there wouldn't have been any in the empty carton. So how did that happen? When? And also, where? In other words, did the murderer stand by Elaine's front door and stir this stuff in? Wouldn't that have been a little obvious? I mean, what if she had come home? Or if someone else had shown up?"

"Best guess? Prepared in advance," he said. "Substituted."

"So did anybody miss a carton of cottage cheese? Was there

a carton stolen out of someone else's delivery? Or out of the truck?"

"Nope. Not on that route."

"Are you sure?"

"Yeah."

"So the murderer had to be one of Jim's customer's. Or somebody on some other route? Anyway, somebody who gets milk delivered, not necessarily in Cambridge, but somewhere, because they don't sell that kind of cottage cheese in stores. I told you that. It's just Pleasant Valley. Was Donna Zalewski on Jim's route? Did she get milk delivered, too?"

Kevin nodded.

"And who else did? Did that woman with the garden? Mrs. Green?"

"Nope."

"Well, who did?"

"Every last damned person who knew Elaine Walsh," Kevin said. "And a lot of people who didn't."

Joel Baker? I'd seen the glass Pleasant Valley milk bottles in that nearly walk-in refrigerator. The Mosses? They must be on Kevin's list of last damned people, along with a lot of others.

The Observatory Hill branch of the Cambridge Public Library is located on Concord Avenue almost directly across from my house, in one corner of the new Harvard town-house complex. Rita had let me borrow one of Elaine Walsh's books. I checked out another. I read some more of what Elaine had written about marriage. I tried to read from Sheila Moss's point of view. And, little as I knew it, from Ben Moss's.

It was necessary, Elaine wrote, for men to become, at most, incidental to women's lives. For a woman to occupy the center of her own life, men had to move—or be shoved—to the periphery. Presence was power, Elaine thought. To gain power, women had to accept anger and destruction and to use both. More than other feminists I'd read (not many), she seemed to have little patience with women who were trying to work out compromises between the past and the future. If I'd been Sheila Moss, I thought, I'd have felt scorned. And Ben Moss? From what Kevin had said, Ben Moss had probably thought she was a hellcat.

Chapter 17

"DID you know Elaine Walsh?" Sheila Moss was holding a carton of Pleasant Valley cottage cheese.

I must have jumped. "Yes. Not too well. I'd just met her."

A few unsubtle questions to Jim, the milkman, had let me time my visit to Sheila Moss to coincide with the Pleasant Valley delivery. I don't think Jim noticed anything, though. By this time, questions about his customers' consumption of cottage cheese must have sounded as novel as "Hot enough for you?" The pretext for my visit was to take some photos of the Ridgeback, Id, who was curled up in a giant wheaten knot, asleep on the linoleum. The dog and the floor could both have used soap and water. Sheila was stowing the Pleasant Valley delivery in a scratched avocado refrigerator plastered with non-representational finger paintings that curled stiffly at the edges. At the bottom of the refrigerator door, someone had used multicolored magnetic alphabet letters to spell out "Josh Moss is a shit." The Mosses must have believed in letting their children express themselves.

"Well," said Sheila, "the oddest thing about Elaine's death was that Elaine really did not like cottage cheese." She was on her knees cramming nearly every kind of product Jim sold into the open refrigerator, shoving six half-gallon glass bottles of milk onto the top shelf and jamming yogurt, sour cream, and a couple of the one-pound cartons of cottage cheese on top of foil-wrapped dishes on the lower shelves. I'd already watched her stash three gallons of ice cream in the freezing compartment. "She didn't like any of this stuff," Sheila added, pointing to the cartons. "Yogurt. White food."

"You know what surprised me?" I said. "I guess I was surprised that she was cooking anything. Somehow, I didn't think of Elaine as somebody who'd cook. She didn't seem domestic. I guess I would've thought she'd live on Lean Cuisine."

"You're wrong," Sheila said. She wore a dashiki over an unironed denim skirt, and red wool socks under the Birkenstock sandals. The hair on her legs was long and dark. "She believed in self-sufficiency, independence. Really, if you ask me, she was something of an isolationist. She wrote about it somewhere. Cooking, I mean."

"A cookbook?" New Ways with Prairie Oysters? But, of course, I'm too much of a lady to have spoken the words.

Sheila laughed. "No. She wasn't that great a cook. It was something about women not taking care of themselves, not feeling worth the trouble. That women cook for men and children, and if we're alone, we don't bother, as if we're not people who need, or maybe deserve, to be fed and . . . to be nurtured. If we don't have somebody else to take care of, we don't take care of ourselves. But she cooked with it? It was in something? That makes more sense, I guess. Fruit salad?"

"Some kind of casserole. Something like lasagna."

"Where did you hear that?"

"Someone told me."

"Huh. You know, she bought it for the dog. When I heard how she died, my first thought was someone had tried to kill her dog, not her."

"Really?"

"Yes. Ben and I both wondered. He and Elaine were very close friends, you know."

To cover my discomfort, I reached down and rubbed the comatose Ridgeback's velvety head. He didn't wake up.

Sheila went on. "Ben has a lot of women friends. I call them his harem." She laughed. "But Elaine was the closest of all. Actually, it was a bit of a problem for me. You want some coffee? It's caffeinated. It's one of the things I live on."

"Sure," I said.

A Mr. Coffee machine spattered with off-white bits of dried batter and whipped cream, I guess, sat on one of the counters. Like everything else in the kitchen, it was surrounded by stacks of opened mail, magazines, newspapers, leaflets, new plastic toys, mixing bowls, paper bags, and the artwork of untalented children. Sheila filled one of the chipped pottery mugs for herself and another for me.

"Sugar?" she offered.

"Please."

I should have said no. She located an empty sugar canister and an empty sugar bowl and had to search through a couple of crammed cupboards before she found a whole-food product called Sucanat. "It's not exactly like sugar," she said apologetically as she put the box on the table and finally sat down, "but it's not too bad. It's very sweet."

Sweet? It tastes like saccharine-laced molasses, but I guess you have to suffer to be natural.

"Anyway," Sheila continued, "Elaine was so active. And she and Ben were always after me to do something with the women's movement. And to read more." She reached over to a counter and pulled out what looked like a thin tabloid newspaper. "Like this. *The Women's Review of Books.* Ben gave it to me for Christmas." She sounded arch.

Cambridge has a lot of men like that. Twenty years ago, I'll bet, the ones like that took their dates to an antiwar rally and a Black Panther breakfast instead of to the theater and a restaurant. Now they whisper in your ear about doing their fair share of the housework, and instead of sending long-stemmed roses, they send you a gift subscription to *Off Our Backs.*

Sheila continued. "And I did look at the first issue, but I haven't even had a chance to open the others. The problem is, really, that I'm not very organized."

"But you have an awful lot to do," I said. "You've got your job and the children and the dog and the house and everything."

"Some people manage," she said. "Or it seems to me that they do."

Car doors slammed, and I heard the sound of high-pitched voices outside.

"There they are," Sheila said. "Now, if the cat will just show up, you'll be all set."

The pretext for my visit was a photo of the Ridgeback with the Moss children and the family cat. Sheila had told me that the dog and the cat were such good friends that they often curled up and slept together. It had seemed to me, so far, that sleeping was Id's almost exclusive activity, but as the voices grew closer, he slowly raised his head and thumped his long tail on the floor in what was evidently, for him, a drumbeat of excitement. Then he rose slowly and padded to the door.

The Moss children, four boys, ranged in age from about seven down to maybe two. The three youngest had on unzipped parkas with mismatched mittens dangling from clips on the sleeves, polo shirts, and Oshkosh overalls, but the oldest had graduated to jeans and gloves. All four looked like their father, who followed them in, and all five big-boned, robust males looked nothing like Sheila, who was frail, haggard, and pasty. No one said hello to the dog or patted him, but he kept wagging his whip of a tail, anyway.

Ben Moss was tall, with thick, curly brown hair showing none of the gray that streaked Sheila's. The features visible above his full beard were heavy but not unattractive, except for his small, cold blue eyes. What struck me most about Ben and the boys, though, was the high color that gave all of them the air of energetic health that Sheila lacked. The Moss family looked as if every day or so, Sheila transfused a couple of pints of blood to her husband and sons.

"Holly," she said. "Ben. This is Holly Winter. She's doing the story about Rhodesian Ridgebacks. And she wants to take some pictures of Id with the boys. And Adler, if she shows up."

Ben Moss looked straight at me, said nothing, and then walked out of the kitchen. The oldest boy opened the refrigerator. The youngest climbed into Sheila's lap and said something I couldn't understand. She lifted up the bottom hem of the dashiki, and he stuck his head under. She was letting him nurse.

"I'm not supposed to let him do this," she said to me. "I'm on Prozac. But he doesn't do it very often."

In Cambridge, people will tell you that they're on Prozac as readily as people in normal places will admit that they're on Weight Watchers. Mothers here no more hesitate to nurse their babies in public than they hesitate to go out in public without veils over their faces. But most nursing mothers here won't even take aspirin or decaf coffee, or if they do, they don't let on.

The nonnursing boys dropped their parkas on the floor and barraged Sheila with protests about everything their father had refused to buy them at the Aquarium. The dog curled up on the parkas and fell asleep. I envied his oblivion. When Ben

Moss stomped back into the kitchen, he didn't even bother to look in my direction. He first complained to Sheila about a bad smell in the bathroom and then said, "Haven't you started lunch yet? What've you been doing all day?"

I wanted to vanish. Failing that, I managed to awaken Id and lure the boys outdoors with him to pose for pictures.

That afternoon, the temperature went up to fifty-five, the sky turned blue, and Steve and I took all four dogs to the Middlesex Fells to let them run. We had to take separate cars, of course, but once we were far enough into the woods to turn them loose, they got along pretty well, which is to say that Lady, Steve's black and white pointer bitch, treated Kimi like God. It suited Kimi fine. India, his German shepherd, alternated between snarling at Kimi and keeping her distance. Rowdy and India were no problem. In fact, they were an ideal pair to take for a walk in the woods because they'd follow each other, and since Rowdy had the sled dog's preference for trails and India always came when she was called, we never had to worry about losing them. I described my morning with the Mosses. Emphatically.

"Would you calm down?" Steve said. "Marriage doesn't have to be like that."

"It's monstrous. And he is the rudest man I think I've ever met. Do you know that the whole time I was there, he didn't address a single word to me? All four of these dogs have better manners than that. Even Kimi."

"At least he wasn't hustling you."

"Just wait. He'll probably call me. He probably thinks he's the strong, silent type and that he made a big impression."

"He'd be right."

"What a bastard! You know, if he wants to be rude to me, fine. I don't care. I can handle it. But how could he do that to her? I was a guest of hers. I was in their house. She tried to introduce us. She must've felt so embarrassed. I felt humiliated for her, to have someone treat her like that. Or maybe she's so beaten down that she doesn't even notice it anymore."

Ahead of us, Rowdy and India were dashing after each other on the path, shiny, beautiful wolflike athletes, but Lady hadn't moved more than a few yards from Steve, and Kimi was devoting herself to provoking Lady's gestures of adulation.

"She's like an overworked dog," I said. "Compared to her, Lady is a model of self-confidence and assertion. It's pathetic."

"I believe you. And did you learn anything?"

"Did I learn anything? Yes. I learned that Elaine was right."

"You know what I mean. And remember, I'm not Ben Moss."

"I know. I'm sorry. In a way, I did learn a few things. Mostly, it's just impossible that Sheila Moss had anything to do with it. For one thing, she's the most harmless person I've ever met. But mostly, she's too disorganized and overwhelmed. Stuff is spilling out all over everywhere. It's completely impossible to imagine her planning anything, never mind murder. And they do get cottage cheese, but she knew that Elaine hated it. She volunteered that. I didn't ask. She also knew that it was for the dog. And I also found out she takes Prozac."

"Didn't you say she was nursing a baby?"

"It isn't exactly a baby. It probably weighs a third of what she does."

"If she's nursing a baby while she's on anything, then she's doing harm to someone," Steve said.

"That's different. The whole situation is just beyond her. Planning to murder someone must give you a sense of power. It's a way of controlling what happens, right? A terrible way, sure, but it must make people feel powerful. And, believe me, she doesn't. She just couldn't do it."

"What about him? Is he enough of a bastard to murder two women?"

"I think he's more of a vampire. He keeps them half alive. Seriously? Mostly, he was Elaine's lover, and he's an M.D. He could've made her death look like suicide. He could've done that easily. Doctors get drug samples all the time. He could've fed her anything he wanted and left a pile of empty bottles or packages. And what's his motive? Before I met them, I thought it was possible that Elaine had threatened to tell his wife. But so what if she had? This poor woman wouldn't have been able to do anything about it if she'd known. What's she supposed to do? Leave him and be stuck with those horrible kids? Anyway, I don't think she knew, from the way she talks about Elaine. I'm sure she didn't. He's given her some kind of line about his friendships with women, and she's bought it. But so what if she'd learned about it? If there's one thing she's not, it's a threat to anyone."

"No one else had such easy access to the Sinequan, you know. He did. She did."

"Not quite. No one else that we know of."

Chapter 18

"THERE'S Catamount and Samuel Adams in there," I said. "Help yourself."

"What's-his-name finished off the Bud?"

Kevin knows Steve's name.

"No one finished it off. No one touched it. It's in there somewhere."

"You got something against dogs all of a sudden? You don't like Spuds MacKenzie?"

"He's all right," I said. "But I don't see why they didn't use a malamute. Rowdy and Kimi would make beautiful mascots."

"For what? Eskimo pies?"

"Ha-ha."

Kevin flipped the top off a can of Bud, leaned against the kitchen counter, and reached over to hand me a photocopy from a machine that needed toner. "Tell me what you make of this."

I'm not sure whether I believe in graphology as a key to character, but if I'd had to make a guess about Donna Zalewski's handwriting, I'd have been wrong. Even in the light copy, it looked flowing, confident, and conventional, like a sample for fourth graders to emulate.

Dr. Walsh—
    I know this is a lot to ask, but I just can't get it under control, and I've tried all the other options, and I know she'll be safe with you. She deserves better than me.

"You got some opinion on that?" Kevin asked.

"This was supposed to be a suicide note?"

"That's what they tell me."

"Then why didn't she sign it?"

He took a sip of beer, pulled his lips shut, and looked at me. I answered him. "Because she never finished it. Other options, huh? I can see that. All she meant were kennels, you know. She didn't mean options in life. You guys have spent too much time in Cambridge. So where'd they find the note?"

"On her desk."

"Was this all?"

"That was the only page."

"There must've been something else," I said. "Instructions. Something about Kimi. When to feed her. Something like that."

"A list," he said. "Basically, she packed the dog's bags. One bag, it was—some kind of canvas gym bag, dog dish, bag of food. A leash. And a list."

"And on the list was what to feed her when, right? And one of the things was cottage cheese."

Kevin nodded.

"So all you want from me is confirmation? Yeah. It's a note asking Elaine Walsh to take care of Kimi. It's an unfinished note. What's missing is something like, 'I'll pick her up tomorrow' or 'I'll pick her up as soon as I get myself together.' "

"You got some ideas on the other options?"

"If that's what you want," I said. "Sure. Where would she have tried to board Kimi? With Steve. Steve was her vet. Another? Faith Barlow. She bought Kimi from Faith. You want me to ask? No one at Steve's will remember, you know. If she called there, which she probably did, she'd just have asked if they could board her dog. If there wasn't room, she wouldn't even have left her name. But Faith might remember. You want me to find out?"

"Naw," Kevin said. "I'm not looking for anything you might call evidence. I just wanted a wild guess."

It's no use answering him when he's in that kind of mood. I picked up the phone and dialed Faith's number.

"Faith? Holly. Listen, did Donna Zalewski ever ask you to board Kimi?"

"I never did," Faith said. "She called once, but I was full up."

"Do you remember when that was?"

"A while ago."

"Can you be a little more specific?"

"Sometime in the fall."

"Do you remember how come you were full? Was something special going on?"

"Oh, yeah. I know when it was. I had a litter almost ready to go, and I was keeping one. Kerry. But I was still calling him Zippy then. And then I got a dog returned. That practically never happens to me. A littermate of Kimi's, actually." Faith was about to tell me everything about that dog and the fate of the rest of the litter, as well as all about why the dog had been returned, and how Kerry was turning out.

"When exactly was that, Faith? Can you give me a month? A day?"

She told me all about why the dog had been returned, why she should never have sold it to the people in the first place, and why she'd sold it to them, anyway, but eventually, she came up with a rough date: Thanksgiving.

By the time we finished catching up, Kevin was on another Bud.

"I suppose you were listening," I said to him. "Is Thanksgiving about right? Does it fit?"

It must have. He got Faith's address and phone number from me, and I don't think it was because he was planning to buy a dog from her. Then he finished his beer and left.

"Men are all the same," I said to the dogs, who were woo-wooing at me for their dinner. Dogs, of course, are entirely apolitical, and one of the many joys of dog ownership is that you can say absolutely anything to dogs without having to consider what they think of you for having said it. Furthermore, you can express one opinion today and another tomorrow, and they'll never point out that you've contradicted yourself. "Get what they want and take off. Did Kevin bother to ask why Donna wanted to find a place to board you, Kimi?"

Her ears pricked up.

"Of course not. But we know. In fact, we understand quite a lot. We probably understand more than we want to. But about Donna? Didn't I tell you she loved you? You know what happened? She told Elaine Walsh. That part of what she told

Elaine was true. She told her about what she was doing to you. She wanted to stop. She loved you. Right?"

The dogs had their eyes on me. It was a few minutes before five. Under no circumstances is their dinnertime earlier than five. They pretend to want dinner whenever they're bored, but I don't give in, because what dogs value most—even more than dinner—is predictability. Who can blame them? People are the same way. For instance, when I meet a married couple, I like to be able to predict that the husband is male, the wife female. Gender itself doesn't matter. What counts is being able to anticipate it.

"You guys are great listeners," I said. "So listen. Donna couldn't get it under control. So until she could, she had to protect you. She tried to find a place to board you, just for a few days, I bet. She calls Steve's, and there's no room. She calls Faith. No go. She probably tries a couple of other places. But you know what? You know why there was no room at the inn? It wasn't Christmas. It was Thanksgiving. Half the dogs in Boston were being boarded because some people's stupid idea of celebrating a holiday is locking their best friends in jail."

The dogs wooed at me.

"So she's desperate. Maybe she feels she's going to pieces. Maybe she's afraid she'll really hurt you this time. She needs help. And she decides to ask the person who's supposed to help most, and that's her therapist, Elaine Walsh. She packs you a suitcase, and she starts to write a note. And that part of the story ends there, guys, because she never finished it. Why? Because she'd just had her dinner, or whatever meal it was. And whatever it was, it was cottage cheese. So maybe she was going to leave you tied outside Elaine's house, or maybe in the waiting room at her office. We don't know. And how come we don't know? Because somebody killed her. And I wish it had been somebody I don't know. I wish it had been somebody who doesn't love dogs. But who else could it have been? Lots of people might have wanted Elaine dead. Ben Moss? Sheila? Antifeminists, like the guy in Montreal? I don't think so, you know, but it's possible. But Donna? Donna was no threat to anybody. Except Joel. He's the only one. He's the only one who had a reason to want them both dead. And I didn't say a word to Kevin, did I? Dinnertime?"

Rowdy had known the word for a long time, and Kimi had

learned it quickly. With Kimi leashed to the knob of the kitchen door and Rowdy on a down at the opposite end of the room, I measured out their Eukanuba. Then I put Rowdy's bowl on the living room floor, released him, got out of the way, and closed the door after him. Kimi was, of course, wooing and yipping, but the second the bowl was within reach of her mouth, she quit it. Her bowl was half empty before it touched the floor. When it did, she lay down flat, wrapped her pretty white forelegs around the bowl, and rapidly finished the food, stopping only to glance up and make sure that I didn't intend to filch any.

"A lot of people believe that a leisurely dinner hour is good for the digestion," I told her.

I picked up her empty bowl and let Rowdy back into the kitchen.

"We don't have to do anything, you know," I said to them. "And one thing we are definitely not doing is going to Kevin Dennehy. But we do have to do something. If it had only been Elaine? I'm not sure. But Donna? Now we know for sure. She didn't want to die. She wanted Elaine to dog-sit. And maybe with Elaine, he really didn't have any other choice. But Donna? He knew she was lying, and she did, too. That's what I don't get. Not really. Couldn't he have talked to her? Okay. Elaine might not have listened. But Donna? Couldn't he have talked to her first? Do we know he didn't? Yes, we do. I think. I think she would've told Elaine. And Elaine would've said something in that second letter. Or there would've been another letter, wouldn't there? You know what I really think? I think Donna would've been relieved. She would've been glad to be talked out of it. She would've been happy to have to tell the truth."

I sat on the kitchen floor and tapped on the linoleum, a signal to Rowdy to join me. He lay down, and I rubbed his ears and ran a finger up and down his muzzle and in the furrow between his eyes. Then Kimi lay down with us, and I started patting each of them with one hand.

"But she never had a chance," I said. "I guess he was just too scared that it wouldn't work. That people would eventually find out about him. He wasn't willing to take the risk. If it had just been Elaine? I don't know. But it wasn't. Maybe he had a good enough reason to kill Elaine. Maybe that was a strange kind of self-defense. Donna? He killed Donna, too. That time,

I think, he had a choice, and what he chose was murder. And if he was scared enough to do that?"

Kimi didn't like having me stare directly into her eyes, but I did, anyway.

"This is partly your fault, you know," I told her. "I wasn't the only one who saw what you did. Other people noticed your bad manners. Joel saw, too. And they saw how embarrassed I was. And they know me. They know I love dogs. And they know I speak dog. Thanks to you, pretty Kimi, he knows I know. He saw how I looked at him."

Chapter 19

"My name is Holly Winter. I'd like to make an appointment with Dr. Arsenault."

"And what is this about?" The woman's voice was so nasal that if Erich Arsenault, M.D., had been an ear, nose, and throat specialist or an allergist, she'd have lost him a lot of potential patients.

What was it about? Well, before I go to Joel Baker and tell him I think he murdered two women, I'd like to know whether he could have got hold of a lot of Sinequan.

"I haven't been feeling too well," I said.

"Then it's not something urgent?"

"It's not really an emergency, but I'd like to see him soon, if that's possible." I wasn't sure how to feign Sinequan deficiency, but I tried to sound depressed and anxious.

"We have a cancellation tomorrow at two-thirty. How's that?"

"Fine," I said.

The next afternoon, I followed her adenoidal directions north up Mass. Ave. past Route 16 and into Arlington, which is a blue-collar city with professorial and professional enclaves. Dr. Arsenault's office wasn't in one. His building was a pale gray, cranberry-trimmed wooden two-family that had been broken up into suites. According to the sign out front, it housed an insurance agent, a podiatrist, and a pediatrician as well as the notorious Dr. Feelgood, although the sign didn't call him that.

Since I hadn't been sure how to look depressed, I'd borrowed one of Rita's books and followed the instructions, which weren't, I think, meant as such, but were helpful, anyway. I hadn't showered or done my hair, and I'd left my face Boston-winter pale. I'd practiced letting my shoulders sag. If you own two Alaskan malamutes, it's almost impossible to get the spar-kle out of your eyes, but I did my best. The anxiety was real. M.D.'s make me nervous because I don't think they're very smart. Suppose you're an intelligent person who decides to enter medicine. Do you confine yourself to one species? No. You trust yourself to cover the spectrum. You become a vet. But if you know you're not bright enough, you go to human medical school. The members of my species have to consult you once in a while, but I do it as seldom as possible.

Dr. Arsenault's waiting room looked almost reassuring. It had the same kind of urine-resistant linoleum and plastic-cushioned benches that you see at animal clinics, but I wasn't fooled. I'd seen the No Dogs and No Bare Feet signs on the outer door.

The origin of the voice was a thin-lipped mouth with red lip-stick serving as a crack-filler, surrounded by several acres of unfilled cracks, a nose both fat and beaky, and eyes so buried in folds that it was impossible to see their color, but her hair was a definite fuchsia, except for the two white inches at the roots. I couldn't see much more of her. She was sitting at a desk behind a high counter. I walked up to it and told her that I had an appointment. She handed me a long medical history form on a clipboard and asked me to fill it out.

I wrote that I'd had a variety of childhood illnesses that I probably did have, even though they went unrecognized be-cause golden retrievers don't get them. Everyone gets chicken pox. I must have. When I did, my parents probably decided that the spots were the first sign that I was finally about to de-velop a respectable coat.

When the form asked whether I'd ever been in psychother-apy and, if so, with whom, I said yes and wrote in Rita's name. The last question asked who'd referred me to Dr. Arsenault, and I was relieved to have a chance to tell the truth. More or less. Dr. Joel Baker, I wrote.

I suppose I must have expected Dr. Arsenault to look and act like a drug-crazed merry prankster who'd giggle like the Maharishi Mahesh Yogi or else like the kind of candy-proffering stranger other people's mothers warned them about. (Mine, of course, warned me never to take a dog from a strange man.) In any case, I didn't expect what I found, an ordinary-looking middle-aged man with tufts of white hair sprouting from his ears and nostrils and a potbelly testing the buttons down the front of his white coat. He didn't giggle or offer me a dog, but he did ask me to remove my clothes. It took me a second to remember that he was, in fact, a doctor and that his request wasn't necessarily an announcement of molestful intentions. He handed me a large piece of blue paper that unfolded into a disposable gown, told me to put it on, and left the examining room.

When he returned, he was holding the form I'd filled out. He must have read Joel Baker's name, but he didn't ask me anything about Joel. All he asked was what the problem seemed to be. His voice was soft and sympathetic. He sounded so nice that I almost told him he should have had more self-confidence and gone for his D.V.M., but I remembered in time why I was there.

"I haven't been feeling so well since my mother died," I said. "And then I lost my dog, and ever since then I've been kind of shaky and nervous. And I haven't been sleeping very well." Well, I do miss my mother. And Vinnie.

He tilted his head, made a couple of quiet clucks, and nodded.

"Well, let's see what's going on," he said.

Although I'd gained the impression from Rita that all he did was write prescriptions, he seemed competent enough at taking blood pressure. Mine, he said, was low. That was good, he reassured me. My pulse was slow, my lungs clear, my heart murmurless. Nothing was enlarged. My problem was stress.

"Stress," I repeated.

"Get dressed, and we'll talk about it," he said.

Only as I was wadding up the blue paper and getting my clothes back on did I realize that he was utterly sincere. In a way, that's what was dangerous about him, I thought. I'd expected a self-defined pill pusher with no pretensions or some charlatan who'd do a cursory physical to remind himself that he was still a real doctor. I'd found, it seemed to me, a sweet man who wanted people to feel better.

When he returned, he asked if I'd ever used Valium, and I said it made me feel depressed. Maybe he'd never heard of

Prozac. The office wasn't exactly trendy, and neither was he. He wrote a big prescription for Sinequan.

When I got back to the waiting room, the nasal voice asked me to pay before I left. Maybe after Dr. Arsenault's patients filled the prescriptions and started swallowing, they became too euphoric and mellow to worry about opening the mail and paying bills. The fee was exactly three times what my first-rate Brigham and Women's gynecologist charges, and she has to pay rent on Francis Street in Boston. Maybe Dr. Arsenault knew, after all. Maybe he didn't. I suspected that most of his patients didn't care one way or the other. I was pretty sure that Joel Baker hadn't.

Chapter 20

"WHAT the hell is this?" Rita waved the prescription form at me. She's been trained to notice everything, I guess. I'd dropped the damned thing on the kitchen counter. She went on. "I don't know why the hell I ever mentioned this bastard's name to you. And once you had it, all of a sudden dogs weren't quite as therapeutic as you always thought. And you couldn't come to me and ask for a referral?"

Rowdy and Kimi, who assumed that anything dangled in the air above their heads should be instantly snatched and swallowed, were circling around Rita like anomalously furry gray sharks about to strike.

"You'd better quit that or feed them," I said, but she ignored me. "And he's not such a monster."

"You don't clean up after him. I've treated at least three people who've been addicted to Valium, thanks to him. You know what he told them? It's like a vacation. That's one of his favorite lines. You need a month in the Caribbean, and here's the next best thing. And he never said anything like 'Use it when you need it.' Oh, no. He had them taking it first thing every morning."

"He's nice," I said. "Rowdy, down. Stay." His legs went out from under him, and he hit the floor. A fast drop is highly desirable, especially once you're in Open, where he and I were headed. "Did you see that? That was lovely. Have I told you that there's never been a C.D.X. malamute in Massachusetts?" Companion Dog Excellent, of course. "We'll probably be the first."

She held up the prescription. "Nice! For God's sake."

"You know, I'm not sure he understands what he's doing.

I think he wants to help, in a weird way. I'm telling you. Before I met him, I expected some kind of fiend, but he isn't. He has a very gentle manner."

"You haven't seen the consequences," Rita said. "They are not gentle."

"He does charge an awful lot of money."

Rita took in a big breath and blew it out emphatically.

"I was wondering if that went up," I said. "Does he keep raising the fee? I read about that somewhere. That once people are addicted, the cost keeps going up. Before I knew how much it was going to cost, I thought, well, he's just sort of misguided. Irresponsible. Not malevolent. But when I found out what it cost, I did wonder."

"No," she said. "He's not one of those. In fact, he makes it easy."

"Maybe the fee goes down. Maybe he charges more for the initial visit. You know, he actually did do a physical. I'm in great shape."

"You didn't go there for this, did you?" She waved the prescription at me again.

"Oh, yes, I did. And I got exactly what I wanted. I found out how easy it was. Anyone could do it. And if you don't quit waving that around, Kimi's going to grab it and take one of your fingers with it."

She dropped the prescription back on the counter. "If you're thinking about Joel Baker, you're wrong."

"I wish you were right."

She shook her head, and her hair moved in a smooth mass, like the coat of a perfectly groomed Shih Tzu. "Joel referred me one of these people. And we've talked about it, including the fact that there wasn't a damn thing we could do about it. We're both Ph.D.'s, and Arsenault is an M.D. So we're not exactly in a position to do anything about him, no matter what he does, because he's an M.D. and we're not. Anyway, Joel had a woman in treatment with him where it was a big problem, because this bastard Arsenault was always available. Things got tough, and all she had to do was see him, and she was in a fog half the time. Joel would never, ever go to him. Not under any circumstances. Not for anything."

"All you're telling me is that he knew where to go, you know," I said.

Rita left angry.

If it hadn't been for my dogs, I might have written to Joel, but how do you justify that to an Alaskan malamute? To two of them? By this time, Rowdy was civilized enough not to hurl himself into the middle of trouble, at least when he was on lead, but the impulse was still there, and Kimi, of course, was a barbarian. "Well, I didn't want to have to face him," I could say to them, but even if I didn't tell them, they'd smell it on me and never respect me again. One of the survival instincts bequeathed to malamutes by their Arctic heritage is a nose for weakness. The scent of cowardice is as appetizing to them as the odor of raw steak, and they take advantage of any sign of it. Writing to Joel would have earned me instant demotion in our pack hierarchy from the alpha leader to the lowliest beta. I'd have deserved it. Alaskan malamutes are often right.

I kept my eyes fixed on them while I made the phone call. They were both curled up on the kitchen floor, their big necks curved, their long-furred tails draped protectively near their noses in case the temperature dropped to sixty below. A short tail is a serious fault in the breed. Rowdy and Kimi both looked ready for a cozy night northeast of the Kotzebue Sound. Even asleep, they set a good standard for me. If serious trouble were to awaken them, they'd go for its throat.

A trick I learned from trying to reach Rita is to call about five or ten minutes before the hour, when a therapist is apt to be between clients. It worked.

"Joel? Holly Winter. I need to talk to you about something. It's important. Is there sometime today when we could get together?"

"Absolutely." He didn't ask any questions.

We agreed to meet at his office, in the rear of his house, late that afternoon. It occurred to me that he might think I was in trouble myself and seeking his advice, but it seemed simplest just to set up the meeting, not to start it over the phone. Still, it made me uncomfortable to realize that if I'd really been in trouble and had called to ask for help, he'd have found that time for me, quickly and unconditionally.

It was one of those sunny, blue-skied Cambridge winter days

that promise April from indoors and feel like a plunge into the Atlantic off the coast of Maine in January when you step outside. I had on a down vest under my L. L. Bean parka, the Thinsulate gloves Kimi had torn and I'd mended, a woolen hat with a pattern of sled dogs, Ragg wool socks, and heavy boots, but no long underwear, and the wind cutting through my jeans drove zero degrees down to thirty below. My eyes watered, my nose ran, and I swore a lot. It was no day for a walk. The Bronco has a good heater, but the car still hadn't begun to defrost when I passed Henry Bear's toy shop on Huron and noticed Kelly Baker looking in the window. In a black one-piece snowmobile outfit with the hood pulled up, she looked so much like a snowsuited ten-year-old that I probably would have taken her for one if it hadn't been for the Ridgebacks, Nip and Tuck, standing with her. The heater was just beginning to work when I pulled into a space on Lakeview and turned off the motor.

A gate in the fence opened into a brick path that led down the side of the Bakers' house and around to the back. In place of grass, which would have been brown and yellow for months to come, an English-ivy lawn grew green, at least for Cambridge winter, on both sides of the brick, and some white birches, hemlocks, and low, leafless shrubs with bright red bark added what gardening books always call winter interest. In back of the house, the path widened into a neatly patterned brick terrace with room for a table and chairs or deck furniture, but all it contained was a rough stone bench just right for two people to sit alone out in the cold. I almost turned around.

I might have if Joel hadn't opened a door at the back of the house, smiled, and welcomed me in. He led me down a flight of beige-carpeted stairs, through a small waiting room that didn't resemble Dr. Arsenault's, or Steve's either—no plastic—and into his office. It looked like the living room of someone with good taste, lots of money, and a ferocious cold. I counted four boxes of tissues. I don't usually enjoy being underground—I can wait—but Joel's office had high, clean windows, small-leafed fig trees in big terra-cotta pots, and enough light to assure me that I wasn't interred.

"This is a lovely room, Joel," I said. "It feels above ground."

"Kelly did that. It's partly the light bulbs. She found some special kind. Full spectrum. Something like that."

Whenever Rita sees a movie with a psychotherapy scene, she gets worked up. "This is going to give people such distorted ideas of therapy!" she protests. If the therapist doesn't talk, Rita says, "People will think that therapists don't do anything!" If the therapist says something, she always decides that it was stupid. We saw one movie that showed a male therapist and a woman client sitting close together on a couch. The therapist had one arm thrown over the back of the couch, not around the woman, but Rita was incensed, anyway. That's why I wasn't surprised to find lots of chairs and no couch, even though Rita's own office has one.

Joel took a seat in a navy-blue barrel chair and gestured toward another one. I sat down. The little table between us held a small pottery lamp and a box of Puffs tissues. I wondered whether either of us was going to cry.

"I feel too bad to lead up to this slowly," I said. "I'm not tactful." I handed him photocopies of the letters Elaine had written to him. "I found these. They were on Elaine's hard disk, on her computer. I don't think she had copies anywhere else."

You'd think he'd have had those letters memorized, but he read them, anyway, and while he did, I studied him and wondered why I'd kept referring to him as he and him, even in my talks with myself. Are people who they say they are? Choose to be? If Joel had said he was Queen Victoria, I might have addressed him as Your Highness, but my mind wouldn't have curtsied. On the other hand, if he'd said he was Queen Victoria, I'd have been certain that he was entirely wrong. As it was, too, he hadn't had to declare himself anything. The person reading the letters wasn't a woman who'd told me she was a man. The person felt implicitly male, at least for linguistic purposes. Yet he wasn't. Kimi told me so, and dogs never lie.

When he finished with the letters, he looked directly at me and handed them back. It was hard to imagine myself in his place, but it seemed to me that I would have wanted to tear them up, photocopies or not.

"Mostly, though, there's that incident at the show," I said. "I know that Donna's accusation was something she made up. I know why it had to be. You saw Kimi. I did, too. I understand the bind you were in."

"Do you?" His voice was neutral.

"You must get lonely sometimes."

He smiled. "Not often. I'm not the first, you know."

"Tell me something," I said. "I don't need to know. I'm just curious. How did it start?"

He laughed, and not nervously. "With an error on a college transcript." He sounded warm, as if the memory pleased him. "A typist dropped two letters from my first name. *L. E.* And I've always imagined that once she did that, she must have thought the 'F' had to be 'M.' "

Joelle. But I didn't speak the name aloud. "It could have been a he," I said. "The typist."

"Yes. One shouldn't assume." He smiled.

"You have a good life. You had a lot to lose."

"A good wife." His hands were resting loosely on the arms of the chair. The muscles in his face looked relaxed. Nothing was twitching.

"I like Kelly a lot," I said. "I like you both. And if it had just been Elaine, maybe I could have understood. But it wasn't."

"No. There was Donna, too."

"And with her gone, you thought Elaine—"

He interrupted me. "I hoped so."

"But you underestimated Elaine. You didn't know her very well."

"Hardly at all."

"Yes," I said. "That's right. You couldn't have. But you knew about Dr. Arsenault."

"Everyone does."

"I didn't."

For the first time, his face showed some strong feeling, and his voice sounded sharp. "He ought to lose his license."

"There is one big gap, though," I said. "There's something I don't get at all. What happened with Donna, when she came to see you? When she was in therapy with you, what was it that went wrong? Why did she leave? She must have been furious, to do something so vindictive. There must have been some reason."

"There always is. People always have good reasons."

Rita spouts platitudes, too. It's one of those occupational hazards.

"Fine, but what were hers?"

"Let's say it wasn't my most brilliantly handled case. She

got to me. She was very good at that. And I confronted her about a few things. Much too directly, much too early."

"That's about you. What about her? I've heard a lot about her, but I haven't heard any reasons. I know she picked at herself, pulled hair, you know. She told wild stories. She made crazy accusations. She did a lot of things. I don't understand why. Not the specifics."

He shook his head slightly and kept his lips closed. Then he said, "That's all confidential."

"I don't believe this. You're willing to murder someone, but you're too ethical to talk about her?" Maybe I sounded shrill. Elaine wouldn't have used that word. She would have said that I sounded powerful. I don't think I did.

He nodded, still smiling a little. "Could we get down to business?"

"Sure. I thought I'd ask you how we do this. My next-door neighbor's a cop. He's a friend of mine. This is his case. He's a little, uh, conservative, but he's a good guy. He's a lot better than most. I can go to him, or you can. It'll be better if you do."

"Of course." He didn't look frightened, threatened, angry, defeated, or anything else except something it took me a second to name: proud. "Give me a week. For Kelly."

"A day." That time, I didn't sound shrill.

"Twenty-four hours."

I gave him Kevin Dennehy's name. He promised to write it all out, arrange things, and show up at Kevin's desk. When I left, we shook hands.

Anatomy is destiny? He took it like a man. A woman? A strong woman? A human being. He took it like a human being, maybe too much so. I walked out of his office and along the brick path. I'd confronted him, yet I had an anticlimactic sense that something had failed to happen. As I was about to get into the Bronco, Kelly Baker came running down her front walk. She must have come home while I was talking to Joel. I didn't want to see her.

"Holly, wait a second! I've had these in the freezer for you for a week."

She'd tossed on a parka, but it wasn't zipped. Her gloved hands held a small package wrapped in aluminum foil.

"They're those *petits pains au chocolat* you liked. I was making some, and I saved these for you."

After what I'd just done to her life, how could I accept? But how could I refuse without telling her what I'd just done?

"Thank you," I said feebly.

I took the package and got into the car, but as I was about to pull away from the curb, I heard her calling my name and banging on the passenger-side window. I reached over and opened the door, and she tucked her head in.

"You do know not to keep those where the dogs can get them?"

I nodded. "Yeah. Anyway, nobody'd feed your cooking to a dog. But thanks for the reminder."

Chocolate toxicosis. The February issues of *Dog's Life, DOGworld, Dog Fancy,* and *The American Kennel Gazette* always tell their readers not to share Valentine chocolate with dogs, but sometimes people are careless or forget, and, of course, a few people don't subscribe. Cocoa and chocolate both contain something called theobromine that's poisonous to dogs. Dogs vary a lot in their sensitivity, but a really small amount of chocolate can kill a very sensitive dog. And there's no antidote.

Chapter 21

As I drove home, I wondered about Joel's compliance. He'd taken it like a human being, it had seemed to me. Did I trust him? Almost. Did he trust me?

Or maybe I simply wanted to run away.

Owls Head, Maine, where I grew up and where my father still lives, is only about four hours from Cambridge if you drive fast and don't take a break, which is to say that it takes me a minimum of five hours. I don't have a Dogs on Board sign plastered to my car, but that's how I drive, and although Rowdy has always been an exemplary traveler, never carsick, he'd always needed to stop at least once on the way. But it's an easy drive, I hadn't seen Buck for a while, and he and Kimi hadn't met each other yet.

Before I let myself into my own place, I dashed up the back stairs, banged on Rita's door, told her I was going to take off, and asked her to bring in the milk and the paper while I was gone. She'll even feed dogs if you beg, but don't bother asking her to walk a malamute. Ever since she sprained her wrist when Rowdy bolted after a cat, she won't.

If there's one best thing about having dogs, it's coming home to them. While you're gone, a person may get into a bad mood, have second thoughts about you, start some project you'll only interrupt, or enjoy being alone. A dog is always thrilled to see you. When I unlocked the kitchen door, Rowdy went into the ritual he'd always saved for occasions when I'd been gone for a long time, that is, more than half an hour. He didn't, of course, jump up. I won't allow a dog to jump. He rose to his full height, placed his big feet on my shoulders, and scoured my face with his tongue. It's impossible to have a malamute and a dirty face. I'd already had some success in teaching Kimi that it's bad manners to jump on people, but I hadn't quite made the point that running around a person and jumping up on her back counts, too. That's what she did. After all, she was jealous of the attention Rowdy was getting, and she was my dog, too, and I was happy to see them cooperating in anything, even if they were squishing the chocolate croissants that weren't shaped like crescents.

"Enough!" I said. I shook the dogs off and put the little aluminum-foil package on top of the refrigerator, where they couldn't get it and where I wouldn't forget it when I left for Maine. I wasn't at all worried about the croissants, of course. Kelly had been on the way out the front door within a minute of the time I'd left Joel's office. Joel couldn't possibly have tampered with them even if he'd wanted to. He wouldn't have had time.

Intelligent dogs can sense the human intention to go somewhere, and they're always determined not to be left home. Kimi and Rowdy pranced and sashayed around as I called my father, who answered on the third ring. There was yapping in the background.

"What's that?" I asked. Wolf dog hybrids do not yap.

"What?" he asked.

"The barking."

"What barking?" He wasn't kidding. He doesn't notice yapping and howling any more than most people notice the sound of their own hearts beating.

"There is a dog barking," I shouted. "I can't hear you very well. Are you in the barn?" The barn hadn't been one for a long time. It has indoor dog pens that open onto the outdoor runs, a maternity ward with whelping boxes, a grooming area with a sunken tub so you don't ruin your back bathing the dogs, and a training area with jumps that let you work in comfort all through the winter. My mother did most of the renovation herself. When Cambridge people say things like "We redid the kitchen" or "We built the deck," all they mean is that they spent money, but Marissa did the work on the barn with her own hands. I miss her a lot.

"Why are you shouting?" Buck said.

The dog finally stopped.

"What kind of dog is that?" I asked.

"A terrier cross."

"With?" Crosses are Buck's specialty. Hybrids. But a wolf terrier?

"God knows." When Buck says that about a dog, he means it literally. The books kept by the angels do not, in his view, so much record human good and bad deeds as keep track of canine matings and bloodlines. Buck plans to spend eternity in a shining heavenly library of celestial stud books. The library will, of course, admit angelic dogs. "She's a nice little bitch," he added. He uses exactly the same words to refer to me.

"I'd like to meet her. You want company?"

"Fine," he said, "but the house is a little full at the moment."

"Has someone got my room?"

"A boxer," he said. Someone else might have thought he meant a pugilist. I knew better.

"I don't mind, but Rowdy might have some objections, and Kimi definitely will. Move him out. You haven't even seen Kimi yet."

He'd heard all about her, of course, and he'd been relieved that I was starting to recover my mental health. He was still worried about me, though. Like Faith Barlow, he has doubts about anyone who owns fewer than six or eight dogs. He might not have evicted the boxer from my room if I'd threatened to show up dogless, but for Kimi and Rowdy, he agreed.

After I fed the dogs and washed and packed their bowls, I tossed a lot of polypropylene, wool, and denim into a suitcase for myself. I was in the bathroom packing my toothbrush, toothpaste, and a few cosmetics—all Revlon and Avon, because they don't test on animals—when I heard noise in the kitchen, a loud thump, then a scraping sound.

Dedicated food thievery is a hard problem to eradicate. Most sensible dog owners find it easier to prevent the problem than to cure it. Our wastebaskets have lids. On the lids, we pile additional deterrents. We close doors. We put temptation out of reach. The one thing Rowdy had had consistent success in filching was the sugar bowl, which I kept leaving out on the table instead of remembering to stash in a cupboard. He could pick it up, carry it to one of his dens, and lick it clean without making a sound, and he'd never once even put a chip in it. With some effort, I could have cured him, but I hadn't made the effort. All I'd done was have him checked for diabetes, but he wasn't diabetic, just predatory. When times got tough for the Inuits who gave us the original malamutes, the people themselves were starving, and the dogs had to fend for themselves. If malamutes hadn't been predators, they'd have starved to death a millennium ago. When Rowdy made off with food, I understood, and, as Rita always says, to understand all is to forgive all. She told me that someone named Madame de Staël said that, but I'll bet she didn't repeat it as often as Rita does. Anyway, I assumed that one of the dogs—probably Kimi—had again knocked the spray bottle of water and the coffee can of pennies off the wastebasket lid and was rummaging in the trash. Then I remembered that I'd emptied the wastebasket.

Both of their black noses were buried in the torn aluminum foil. Like a pretty wolf pair enjoying a romantic dinner for two over a caribou carcass, they weren't even fighting over the frozen chocolate croissants. You don't believe in obedience training? Listen.

I walked up to Rowdy. "Rowdy, drop it. Leave it." My voice was quiet, low, and firm. I took his collar in my hand and tugged, just to remind him. He opened his jaws, and a hunk of pastry dropped to the floor. I backed him up a foot or two and said, "Good boy. Rowdy, sit." I put my left hand in front of him with my palm just in front of his face. "Stay."

I had no way to tell my barely Pre-Novice Kimi to stop eating, nothing to offer her that could tempt her away in the next second, no liver in my pockets, no time to raid the refrigerator. I knew she might bite me, but there was no time to run for the leather gauntlets I keep for emergencies. In a second, I was standing over her, one hand grabbing her collar, the other locked over and around her muzzle, my fingers digging hard, forcing her jaws open, forcing her to release her grip on the food. Her jaws began to loosen, and I used both hands to pry them open and shake her head until the chocolate mass fell out and hit the floor with a splat. I got both hands around her collar and jerked her away before she could snatch it up again. She didn't understand, or if she did, she hadn't read Madame de Staël.

With one quick twist of her head, she did what any sensible predator does to a creature stealing its prey: She bit me, and not on my sweater-padded arm or wrist, either. Right on the hand. Rather, right *in* the hand, a quick, clean slash deep into the flesh between the thumb and first finger. If you've never been bitten by a dog, you might imagine that it feels as if you'd been cut with a knife or jabbed with a nail, but a serious bite feels more as if you've been slammed with a baseball bat. The physical pain is intense, but the emotional pain is worse. It hasn't happened to me often, but each time, I've cried. The impossible has transpired. Oh, God. Yes. A dog *will* bite *me*. It was my fault, of course. I should have approached her from the front or side, and I should have kept talking. As it was, she hadn't had a chance to know whose hand she was biting. I even forgave her. I still had my feelings hurt. But I didn't let her go.

The blood flowed all over my hand and dripped down onto Kimi, where some of it sank into the dense coat of gray around her neck and some of it stained her ears. She fought me all the way across the kitchen to her crate, but I shoved her in and locked the mesh door. Then I bled and throbbed my way back to Rowdy, who, I would like to point out, hadn't broken his long sit. Maybe I should have trusted him, but I didn't dare to take the chance. I took his collar in my good hand. "Okay," I told him. "Good boy." Never forget to praise your dog, Marissa taught me. Never. Then I guided him gently across the red-spattered floor, assured him that everything was going to be all right, and shut him in my bedroom.

I talked to Kimi while I stood at the kitchen sink, held the wound under the faucet, and let the hot water flow into it. Rowdy might have understood words, but since Kimi hadn't moved beyond tone of voice, I indulged myself. My voice, though, was calm and soft. "You little fiend," I said lovingly. "This hurts like all hell. You are a damned little monster, aren't you? And if you haven't slashed a tendon, I'm really, really lucky."

After watery red had flowed over the white enamel for a while, I turned off the faucet, put a thick pad of paper towels under my hand, and groped in the cabinet above the sink for a bottle of Betadine left over from some distant veterinary injury, an abscess in the leg of one of the cats, it seemed to me. In back of a compendium of eye ointments, ear drops, heartworm medicine, cotton balls, gauze pads, swabs, rubbing alcohol, and powdered calcium supplements, all pharmaceutical artifacts of dogs and cats I'd owned, I located the bottle. When I held the bleeding hand over the sink again and upended the bottle over the bite, the pain wasn't as bad as I'd expected. Then I piled on some of the gauze pads, added a layer of paper towels, phoned Steve, got his answering service, and insisted that I had an emergency. The operator let me ring through to him.

"It's me," I said. "Both of the dogs ate chocolate. It was my fault. I left the stuff on top of the refrigerator, and Kimi must've climbed onto the counter. Rowdy's never done it before. I think she was the one. Can you get here? Or do you need me to bring them in?"

He hears this kind of thing all the time, of course, and he never panics. He asked how much they'd eaten and whether they were acting nervous, salivating, or vomiting. They weren't. The torn foil was still lying on the floor, thick with crumbs, chocolate, and blood. I didn't even know how many croissants there'd been to begin with, but not many. Two? Three? Nothing was left except foil, crumbs, and the remains they'd had in their mouths.

"It was chocolate croissants," I said. "Maybe one each? But I don't know how much chocolate there was in them." I'd stayed calm with the dogs, but I was starting to sound scared.

"So not much," he said. "Maybe an ounce. First of all, the chances are good that nothing will happen. Some dogs aren't very sensitive to it. And these are big dogs. That's on their side. Chances are you won't even notice anything's wrong. I'm coming over, anyway, and we'll keep an eye on them, but nothing bad is going to happen."

"I trust you," I said. "Just get here fast, would you?"

By the time he arrived, I'd arranged what I thought was a near-professional bandage on the hand, I'd cleaned up most of the mess, and I was sitting on the kitchen floor with Rowdy and telling him not to worry. Kimi was still in her crate. Steve insisted on undoing the bandage, and then we had a fight about M.D.'s. He wanted me to go to the emergency room. I won. He rebandaged my hand.

When he finished with me, he checked on Kimi again. She was asleep. We couldn't wake her up.

Chapter 22

"How much did she swallow? How much was it that actually went down?" Steve always talks slowly and calmly, never more so than in a crisis. His face registers nothing except concern and intelligence, but his eyes turn from blue-green to sea-green.

"I told you. I'm not sure. Not all that much. She couldn't have. Rowdy got some, and the package was small to begin with. I didn't open it, but there couldn't have been more than a few."

"Let me see what's left."

"It's outside in the trash. I took it out to the barrels."

"I'm going to want you to get it. Wrap whatever you can find in a plastic bag. I've got to take her with me. I should've had you bring them in."

With her head at the door of her big tan polypropylene crate, Kimi looked no more than sound asleep, deeply asleep, but her breathing was beginning to sound slow and heavy, at least to me. Or maybe I was listening harder than usual.

"Tie Rowdy up or shut him in the bedroom," Steve added. "We don't need his help right now."

By the time I'd put Rowdy in my room and returned to the kitchen, Steve had eased Kimi out of the crate, and she was lying on the floor, stretched out, not curled up, as if she found herself dead weight.

"Get the doors for me," Steve said. "I'll take her as she is. She's not going to run off anywhere for a while."

After years of hoisting hefty dogs onto exam tables, he'd developed not only muscles but technique as well, and he'd somehow avoided ruining his back. Kimi's seventy-five pounds didn't strain him, and he didn't rush. I opened the back doors, ran down the stairs, and slid open the door on the side of his van. He followed, lowered Kimi gently onto the carpet in back of the driver's seat, and covered her with an old blanket that belonged to India, his shepherd. He sprinkles the van with Nilodor and vacuums it, but it still smelled of dogs and old blankets, even on that cold night.

"Don't wait for me," I said. "I'll be there right after you. I'll just get Rowdy."

"Get him there fast," Steve said, and added, "Whatever's doing this, it isn't chocolate."

Before I went back indoors, I took the lid off a trash can and retrieved the plastic bag containing, among other things, the aluminum foil and half-gnawed globs that the dogs had unwillingly dropped. When I emptied the bag onto the kitchen floor, coffee grounds, eggshells, sodden sheets of paper, wet tea bags, half a moldy cantaloupe, and something that may once have been cheese tumbled out with the foil and pastry. The whole mess smelled like a finger down my throat, and my stomach felt as if I'd eaten three or four large servings of candied yams, but I sorted out the remains that Steve wanted and sealed them in another bag.

Afraid to see what might have happened to Rowdy, I dreaded opening the bedroom door, and when I did open it, my heart started to pound. Rowdy was curled up under the bay window.

"Rowdy, let's go!" I said. "Let's go ride in the car."

He'd understood those words for quite a while, and his usual response to them was to perk up his ears, bounce, twist, and zoom for the door. That night, he opened his eyes, shook his big head a little, and then rested it solemnly on his forepaws. Sadness is a common expression in some dogs, but not in Rowdy or any other malamute. He'd have made a bloodhound look overjoyed.

"Time to wake up," I said brightly. "You've got no choice."

When I held his collar with my good hand and dragged him to his feet, he wagged slowly all over, but not with his usual vigor, and I had to march him into the kitchen. The sight of his leash meant nothing to him, but, outside, the open tailgate of the Bronco did. He tried to jump in, but the energy was missing, and I gave him a boost. I had to use both hands to lift him. The injured one felt as if it would explode. To keep him awake on the drive to Steve's clinic, I never stopped talking, and I used all his favorite words, especially his own name. "Rowdy, watch me. Watch me, boy. Good boy. Let's go. Rowdy, go for a ride? Go for a walk? Rowdy, wake up." But when I parked the car and opened the tailgate, he was asleep.

"Rowdy, wake up! Let's go!" I put my good hand under his chin and lifted up his head. In the dim light from the little bulb inside the Bronco, I watched his eyes lift open, then droop. "You have to wake up," I insisted. "I know you don't want to. You have to, anyway. I can't carry you. You're a lot bigger than Kimi, and my hand hurts like hell. You've got to take some of your own weight." Using my good hand as much as I could, I gripped his shoulders and dragged him toward me until I pulled his forepaws out of the car. Perhaps it was the fear of falling that roused him, but when he shoved with his hindquarters and propelled himself all the way out, he nearly landed on his head, and I had to catch him. That hurt, too. But he was on his feet, supporting himself, and as we made our way from the car to the door of the clinic, he didn't try to lie down.

Steve had used a rubber wedge to prop open the swinging door that separates the waiting room from the corridors and back rooms of the clinic. I led Rowdy through the door. "Steve?"

He stuck his head out through another swinging door and glanced at Rowdy.

"He keeps falling asleep," I said.

"Anything else? Salivating? Vomiting?"

"No. Just sleepy."

"Okay. Stay out here. I'll take him."

"Did you make Kimi vomit?"

"She's too sedated," he said.

"So what do you do?"

"Gastric lavage. Come on, Rowdy."

"Him, too?"

"I can induce vomiting."

I paced the waiting room and studied the poster depicting the life cycle of the heartworm and the framed pieces of Steve's mother's embroidery that I'd always disliked, depressingly in-accurate representations of terriers. Noises came from the back rooms of the clinic, and new smells mingled with the usual ones of dogs, cats, disinfectant, odor-control products, and odors the products didn't control. When Steve brought Rowdy back, they both looked more cheerful than they had. Then Steve returned to Kimi, and I talked to Rowdy. I can never shake the sense that if I pitch and tune my voice to some mysteriously therapeutic key, it'll enter an ailing dog's ears, travel through his nervous system, and heal whatever part is diseased. Rita derides this conviction as an instance of something called preoperational thought, which seems to mean wishful thinking, but it's true that Rowdy got better. From upstairs, India barked, and somewhere at the back of the clinic, a couple of dogs took up her challenge. Rowdy and I both listened. He noticed the barking. His eyes brightened, and the fur on his back rose. His hackles were beginning to go up.

Steve finally reappeared.

"She's weak," he said. "But I think she's going to make it."

"I need to see her."

Kimi lay on her side in a big cage, her strong legs extended, her massive, pretty head resting as if the strength to lift it had deserted her. Dark wolf gray and white is the official designation for Kimi's shade of malamute. It means a guard coat of almost-black with tones of silver and fresh Arctic snow over the thick pile of undercoat, a complex, balanced, and symmetric study in what happens to black, white, and gray when they come to life. On a malamute like Kimi, the dark brown eyes and touches of earth in the coat are somehow unexpected and miraculous, like black-and-white film developed into a color print. When she heard my voice, those dark almond eyes widened, dyspeptically happy.

I opened the cage and stroked her head, smoothing down that cat-soft fur on and around her ears. "So you made it, huh? I get to keep you, after all?"

Vince, our head trainer at Cambridge Dog Training, once said to me, "Holly, if I took a dog into my house, and then all four of its legs fell off, it'd still be my dog." I knew what he meant. The religion in which Buck and Marissa raised me does not recognize divorce. My dog is my dog, till death us do part. Kimi had been mine almost from the second I'd first seen her at Elaine's and wanted a mal just like her. But . . . ? But until Kimi nearly died, Rowdy was more my dog than she was.

Never be afraid to tell your dog the truth. If you don't want to be overheard because you're scared of sounding corny, maudlin, melodramatic, or demented, all you need to do is whisper. Dogs hear better than people do, and they have no fear of elemental truths. I didn't bother to whisper. The only other human being in the room was Steve. "I love you, you old wolf," I told her.

Steve closed the door of her cage and led me back to the waiting room, where we sat on a bench.

"Christ," I said to him. "I never thought they could get to the top of the refrigerator. Rowdy never has. I've always put food there. He's never gone for it."

"There are dogs that walk fences. They can climb ladders."

"I know about chocolate. I've warned people about it. How could I have been so stupid?"

He shook his head gently. "Forget it. I don't know what this is, but I've been through what's left and the, uh, stomach contents." He shrugged. "It's not like they'd raided a box of candy. The books say that eight four-ounce bars of milk chocolate can kill a thirty-pound dog. From cardiac arrest."

"She got to it first, I think. She must have. She must have got on the counter. That's not one of his tricks. And I got to him first. I made him drop what he had in his mouth. I tried to shake what I could out of her mouth, but she swallowed more than he did."

"Not enough. And he's feeling it. There's not a chance they got enough to do this, and the clinical picture's all wrong. The first thing you expect is a nervous, restless dog."

"And they're sleepy."

"Yeah, the opposite. Theobromine's a CNS stimulant, like caffeine. Maybe with a massive amount, you'd see a dog collapse fast, but . . ."

I could hear Kelly Baker's words. *I've had these in the freezer for you,* she'd said. *I saved these for you.*

Kelly? Kelly had watched me eat four of the things. I'm not really greedy. It's just that small portions leave me hungry. I'd had to wonder about the size of the package. After she'd seen me devour four croissants and clean up the crumbs, generous Kelly, who enjoyed feeding people, had given me two or three. Because I wouldn't leave a trace?

Or maybe not Kelly. I could see the doors of the professional, restaurant-size refrigerator and freezer, with their neat, ordered lists. When she put that package in the freezer a week ago, maybe it had my name on it, and she probably added it to the inventory, too. One package of *petits pains au chocolat*. That's what they really were, I remembered—I speak a little French, but not aloud—and that's what she'd have printed carefully on the list on the door. For Holly Winter. Joel would have seen it, or maybe he'd noticed the package itself. My name might have been on that, too. He wouldn't have had time to tamper with it on my last visit. He'd have to have planned it in advance.

But then, it had been Kelly who warned me about the chocolate, who warned me to keep it away from the dogs. She loved dogs. She'd never hurt one. Neither would Joel. And both of them knew me well enough to feel certain I'd never give chocolate to my dogs.

Kelly? Kelly was the cook. She had chosen to use chocolate; in other words, chosen to give me something I'd never feed my dogs. But maybe she'd simply remembered that I'd liked those *petits pains*. She could have mentioned it to Joel. I felt like murdering one of them. Or both? Or only one. But not the wrong one.

I wanted to talk it over with Steve, but he refused to listen. He insisted that he was going to give Rowdy the thorough exam that he'd delayed because of Kimi, and he managed to talk me into going to the Mt. Auburn emergency room, a place I hate.

"It's feeling better already," I said.

"You're lying. The blood's seeping through the bandage."

"I can't stand hospitals."

"They won't keep you overnight."

"Absolutely. Because I won't stay."

"All they'll do is stitch it up."

"It doesn't need it."

He sounded casual. "Of course, if there's a tendon involved or something, you could lose the use of that hand." He was stroking Rowdy's head and looking at him. "Could be permanent. If it gets infected, you'll know, because it'll swell up. And you might not be able to use it for a couple of months. And it'll hurt like hell when anything brushes against it." He kept patting Rowdy.

"I get the point." If *you* don't get it, borrow two malamutes and walk them on leash sometime.

"Of course, you don't have to go," he said. "No one is making you. It's your choice."

Chapter 23

FOR a study in love and terror, go to the emergency room at Angell Memorial or any other big animal hospital. You'll see owners holding cats and dogs, stroking them, and murmuring nonstop. You'll see people who aren't ashamed to sit alone on the wooden benches and let tears wash down their faces.

On the other hand, most of the people waiting at the Mt. Auburn emergency room were reading grubby copies of tabloids, dozing off with half-closed eyes, or just sitting, impassive, almost inanimate. It was hard to tell the patients from the accompanying friends or relatives. A man and woman in their twenties hovered around a little girl and took turns talking to her and feeling her forehead, but the other adults might have been strangers who happened to find themselves on the same crowded subway car. In case anyone needs proof, emergency rooms demonstrate that people care more about their animals than they do about themselves and other adults.

But I wasn't depressed. As I waited on a hard wooden chair with the other commuters, my good hand was in a tight fist, and my jaw was locked. I kept envisioning the pay phone down the corridor. Because I was actually bleeding—in fact, dripping through the bandage—my turn was supposed to come soon. I was trying to decide whether I had time to make the call. I'd begin to stand up. Then I'd decide that I didn't want to be interrupted on the phone or miss my turn, and I'd sit down again.

When my turn finally came, the doctor asked a lot of obnoxious and insulting questions about my dog and wouldn't believe that the bite wasn't her fault. He referred to my gorgeous Alaskan malamute bitch as "your husky." He told me about his allergies and didn't know that dog bites are much less likely to get infected than cat bites. I was glad he hadn't tried to go to veterinary school. I let him stitch up my hand, anyway. When he finished bandaging it and quit polluting my ears with his ignorant antidog drivel, I could hardly wait to get out of Mt. Auburn, but I stopped at the pay phone, anyway.

Thanks to Rita, I am an expert on telephoning psychotherapists. As I've already mentioned, in the daytime, you call five or ten minutes before the hour, when there's a chance that the therapist is between clients. Any other time, expect to get an answering machine, but don't despair: leaving a message on it isn't a waste of time because therapists are always monitoring their messages. They don't want to be interrupted every second, and they think it's neurotic to make themselves available whenever anyone has a breakthrough dream at three A.M., but they don't want to miss real emergencies, either. Rita checks her messages constantly to make sure that none of her clients is in big trouble. Joel Baker probably did, too.

Information gave me two numbers for Joel Baker and none for Kelly. If one woman marries another, doesn't she still need to be a telephonic person in her own right? Anyway, the first number, of course, got me a machine, and Joel's voice said to call the other number in an emergency. I did. I'd have thought that Kelly might at least have left her voice on the second machine, but she hadn't. Furthermore, lots of hard-core dog people (and women who understand what knocks the wind out of a breather) record choruses of barking or howling along with their own voices, but Joel's taped voice was *a cappella*. He gave his name and said to wait for the beep and leave as long a message as I wanted.

I took a big lungful of air. The machine squealed. "This is Holly Winter. I didn't enjoy the chocolate croissants at all." I paused. "In fact, I didn't even taste them. My dogs stole the package. After a while, they fell asleep, and I couldn't wake them up."

I hung up. Let her suffer. Him? They both loved dogs. They both knew mine. Kelly or Joel, one of the two, would feel worse about killing my dogs than about killing two people.

Driving my solid, chunky car through the narrow streets back to Steve's, I thought about calling Kevin Dennehy. The only thing that restrained me was what Joel had been through already. Donna Zalewski and Elaine Walsh had both accused him of something he hadn't done. To defend himself, he'd have had to reveal the great secret of his life, and the revelation would have ruined everything for him, not only his career but his whole place in the world. If people had known, he wouldn't have been Joel Baker anymore. And, of course, Kelly wouldn't have been Kelly. In the eyes of most people, even in Cambridge, liberal heaven, where lesbian couples can live about as openly as they can anywhere, he'd have been a freak, a woman passing herself off as a man. And what would Kelly have been? If the word existed, I'd never heard it. And their marriage? Plainly enough, they wouldn't be married anymore. I thought about some of the lesbian couples I knew. Joel and Kelly weren't one. They weren't and didn't want to be, I thought. They wanted to be man and wife. That's what they were. I'd never thought of them in any other way.

Safe once again in a real medical setting, I found Steve asleep on a fold-out bed in the back corridor. He was lying on his stomach with one arm hanging over the side of the cot and his hand wrapped around one of Rowdy's paws. In some atavistic search for a cave, Rowdy had crawled under the cot, but when I walked in, he removed his paw from Steve's hand, wiggled out, and shook himself awake. Then he deposited his ninety pounds hard on the floor, rolled belly-up, and tucked in his snowshoe paws. If you look like a particularly handsome wolf that bulks up with free weights, it must be hard to put on a convincing pussycat act, and it deserves a reward. I knelt down and ran my good hand over his chest. Then I made my way around the cot, pushed open a door, and found Kimi asleep in her cage. The fur over her ribs was rising and falling slowly and regularly. The black mask around her closed eyes gave her a serious, purposeful expression. She didn't look doped or sick, but intent on working at sleep. One of her back feet twitched, then one ear. What awakened her was not, I think, my presence, but Rowdy's. He mashed his big black nose against the mesh and gave a noisy sniff. Before she even opened her eyes, she lifted her head.

"Would you get him out of there?" Steve looked rumpled. "Let her rest."

"She's okay," I said. "Isn't she?"

He nodded. "They're both fine. She just needs some rest. How's your hand?"

"You have no idea how much M.D.'s don't know," I said. "But I'm okay, anyway. Look, are you awake? I need to talk about something."

Back in the corridor, he folded up the cot and stowed the metal frame in a closet. He and Rowdy and I sat on the mattress on the floor. Rowdy took up most of it.

"I'm trying to decide what to do," I said. "I'm positive that one of the Bakers killed Elaine Walsh and Donna Zalewski. I'm just not absolutely sure which one, and I don't want to turn in the wrong one."

"Both?"

"Oh, both of them knew. I'm sure. That's not the issue. Can I talk it out?"

"Can I stop you?"

Rowdy had his head resting on his forepaws, and he was staring up at Steve, who was running a finger up and down the furrow that malamutes have between their eyes.

"Do you want to?"

"No." Steve has sad eyes.

"Okay. Here's what I think. Donna makes this accusation to Elaine. And you know what? Donna's done this stuff before, and what's happened? Basically, nobody's taken her seriously. Her roommates didn't. And I'll bet nobody else did, either. But this time, it's different. First of all, Elaine is her therapist, and it's her job to take things seriously. Mostly, though, she's telling Elaine exactly what Elaine loves to hear, and that's that she's been abused by a man. If the story she told Elaine had been about something else, Elaine might have realized it wasn't true. Well, Rita would probably say it was, anyway. Emotionally true. That it wasn't historical reality, that's what Rita would say."

"Don't believe everything Rita says."

"She's usually right. In her own way. Anyhow, Elaine was ready to believe it. That's one reason I decided it couldn't have been Ben Moss. It crossed my mind that he could really have seduced Donna, and she could've told Elaine, but that's impossible, because Elaine wouldn't have kept seeing him, and she did. Right to the end. Kevin told me. And about Joel, she didn't want to find out whether it was true. She wanted to believe it. And then she wanted to act. So she writes that letter. Joel reads it. What's he going to do next? Obviously, he has to show it to Kelly, and not just because it threatens her, too, but because he doesn't have anyone else he can tell about it."

"He has to tell someone?"

"He's a therapist. That's how they're wired. No matter what happens, they've got to talk about it. They think privacy is bad for your mental health or something. Anyway, then they both know. And here's what I think happens next. I think that in a way, Kelly responded just the way Elaine did, or sort of. She was the one who wanted to do something. And she was the one who knew something Joel didn't necessarily know, which was about Pleasant Valley. Not only does she walk the Ridgebacks every day, but she walks them probably more than anyone else in Cambridge walks dogs. It can be five below, and you see her out walking them. Everywhere. But especially on Lakeview, of course, because that's where she lives. So naturally, she went by Donna Zalewski's house, which was on Lakeview, too, on the other side of Huron from the Bakers'. And her obvious route over to Brattle Street and the river."

"Wait a minute. How was she supposed to know that's where she lived?"

"More or less the same way I found out. I looked in Rita's Rolodex. She looked in Joel's, only not just in his Rolodex, I bet. In his files, too, I bet. His office is right in their house. I'm sure he doesn't lock her out. She's probably the one who cleans it, or at least takes care of the plants. So she knows where Donna lives, and when she goes by there, she notices the milk box. There isn't one now, but when Donna lived there, it must have been right on the porch. And she could tell it was Pleasant Valley because they all have that picture of the cow on them. And that's how the idea came to her: put something in Donna's milk. Or whatever it was. Maybe it was cottage cheese that time, too. Ice cream. Whatever. And how does she decide what to use?"

"She's read the file."

"That's what I think. In Joel's file on Donna Zalewski, it says she's using Sinequan. Or maybe had used it. And Kelly knows about Arsenault because Joel would've. Joel knows all about him and really hates him. I mean, not personally, I guess, but hates how irresponsible he is. So Kelly did exactly what I did. She made an appointment. He saw her right away. He gave her a whopping prescription with a lot of refills."

"And?"

"And she opens the capsules, takes the powder inside or maybe dissolves the whole thing, and somehow gets it into something in Donna's milk box. I don't know what. I don't know how. And since Donna's taking it, anyway, and since she's more than a little flaky, it works, just as planned."

"Except for Elaine Walsh."

"Exactly. Elaine doesn't stop. So Kelly does a repeat performance. Why not? It worked the first time. Only, of course, Elaine wasn't taking Sinequan, and she wasn't suicidal, and she wasn't writing any letters. My guess is that Kelly hoped it would somehow look like suicide, mostly because she'd have known that Elaine would be depressed about losing a patient. I mean, she'd have known how hard therapists take that. But you know what I think? I think maybe Kelly didn't know how else to murder someone. It's as simple as that. It was the only way she'd ever done it, and it had worked fine that time. Anyway, what happened the second time, with Elaine, is what makes me think it was Kelly, not Joel. Listen."

"I am." He lay down, shoved Rowdy gently to the edge of the mattress, and stretched.

"That time, we know for sure what the stuff was in, right? Cottage cheese. And also, we know it was mixed in. It wasn't just sprinkled on top because there were traces of it in the empty carton. Okay? So there are two possibilities. One, she goes to Elaine's, opens the milk box, takes the top off the carton, puts the stuff in, and pulls out a spoon and stirs it up."

Steve looked skeptical.

"Right," I said. "So the likely scenario is this. She orders cottage cheese from Pleasant Valley. So does Elaine. I'm not sure how Kelly knows, but she does. Anyway, Kelly takes her own carton, doctors it up at home, and when she gets to Elaine's, all she has to do is substitute it. That's all. Open the milk box, take out Elaine's, put hers in. It'd take a couple of seconds."

"Hold it," Steve said. "Why is she messing around with someone's milk box?"

"That's one reason it was Kelly," I said. "Because she's the one who walks the dogs. There's a leash law, right? And she always has Tuck on leash. But not Nip. He just sort of ambles along with her. He doesn't really need to be on leash. I know all dogs belong on leash if they're within a mile of a street. I agree, but she doesn't. Anyway, she carries a leash for him, but he's usually wandering around. So if she's on Elaine's porch? Or, for that matter, Donna's? Well, it's because her dog has gone onto someone's porch, and all she's doing is getting him back. And not only that, she's stopping him from raiding the milk box. It's the perfect excuse. And, of course, the other thing is, she walks those dogs everywhere. All the time. She's like the mailman. Nobody wonders why she's anywhere because she's always around, walking the dogs."

"Doesn't he ever do it?"

"He probably does, once in a while. And on weekends, they both do. They walk them together. But we don't get milk delivered on weekends, not on our route. I'm on the same one. And Joel is working during the week. He's seeing clients. She isn't. She's walking the dogs. Cooking. Doing all the domestic stuff."

"So why not both of them? Even if she's the one who made the delivery, so to speak."

"I'm telling you, it's possible. But she could have done it alone, and he couldn't, also because of the way their kitchen is. It's not a normal kitchen. It's fantastically ordered, like a lesson in domestic science or something. Everything in the freezer and the refrigerator is listed. It's all posted on the outside. If he'd snatched something out of there, she'd have probably noticed. But if she'd taken the cottage cheese . . . ? Look, it's morning. He goes to see his clients. She doctors up the cottage cheese, takes it to Elaine's, substitutes it, comes home, and pops Elaine's cottage cheese in their refrigerator. He wouldn't have known."

Steve nodded.

"But Joel? Suddenly, he shows up in the kitchen, grabs a fresh carton of cottage cheese, runs off with it, mixes in some Sinequan, and announces to Kelly that he's taking the dogs for a little stroll?"

"She could've been out somewhere."

"Absolutely. It is possible. That's why I'm trying to think it out. But the point is, it would've been easy for her, harder for him. And look. This is not a couple that believes in doing everything fifty-fifty. Some couples have two phones because otherwise they fight about how to divide up the phone bill, and if you call the wife at the husband's number, he won't get her and makes you call hers, and vice versa, right? Well, that's exactly what they're not like."

"Yeah, but wouldn't he have guessed something was up?"

"Well, of course he would. He had to know. I don't know that he necessarily knew about Donna. But he had to know about Elaine. I mean, he couldn't possibly have believed that that was just a coincidence. From his point of view, it would've been absolutely too good to be true. He had to figure it out. But what was he supposed to do? That's why he didn't challenge me. That's why he looked proud of himself. Kelly is his wife."

"They're both women," Steve said flatly.

"Not to each other. That's why she killed Elaine. And Donna. Or why they both did. They just wanted to stay who they are."

"So do I," he said. He sat up, took Rowdy's collar, led him into an exam room, and shut the door. Then he came back to the mattress. "And we're not both women."

Chapter 24

AT about five A.M., my heart moved from my chest to my bandaged hand, where it pounded me awake. The airless corridor stank in equal parts of sick dogs and healthy people. Without disturbing Steve, I retrieved my clothes and felt my way to the door to Kimi's sickroom. The early morning light of a bleak, gray day was coming through the windows as I pulled on my jeans and sweatshirt, but no morning is ever entirely bleak and gray when you own a good dog. Kimi did her best to struggle to her feet, made it, shook herself, wagged her long, lovely tail, and wooed softly to me. I opened her cage and let her loose. She was wobbly on her feet, but her spirits were restored.

"Something tells me there's no breakfast for you today," I whispered to her. "Sorry."

I knelt down, and she did her best to get her forepaws around my neck. I had to help her. Then she scoured my face with her wet tongue. Rowdy, who could sense serious competition for my affection even in his sleep, whammed open the swinging door, barged in, and shoved her out of the way.

"Gentle," I told him softly. "Be gentle. Go easy."

I heard Steve mumbling something.

Kneeling on the floor, with my hand pounding, my clothes dirty, my breath foul, and my face early-morning greasy and dog-lick shiny, I felt grubby and oddly clear-headed. I owned the two most beautiful dogs on earth. They were gentle, affectionate, intelligent, and still alive. Their safety freed my anger. Did I have to know which of the Bakers had almost killed them before I did something about it? If I'd almost died, would either of them have stopped to gather information, ponder, and debate? Alaskan malamutes don't start fights. But they never,

ever run away from them, either. I hadn't started anything. Why should I run away? Why should I wait? Imagine an Alaskan malamute giving someone twenty-four hours. The right person? A malamute wouldn't have cared either way. Mostly, though, a malamute wouldn't have delayed for what I suddenly saw as the central reason I'd been so understanding, so compassionate, so timid: A malamute bitch wouldn't have been afraid to confront another female. Malamutes are genuinely unprejudiced, and when they judge, entirely impartial. Unafraid of their own strength, the bitches do not hesitate to take on one another.

My hand hurt like all hell, but the pounding felt more like anger than like pain, the insistent surging of my own strength. But my mind was lucid. No one else had played fair, not Donna, not Elaine, not the Bakers.

An hour later, I was parking the Bronco on Lakeview in front of Joel and Kelly Baker's house. My hair was still wet from a quick shower at home. Something had made me wear black: black jeans, a black cotton turtleneck, a black sweater. In the bathroom mirror, my scrubbed face had looked as white as if I'd powdered it with talc, and I'd left it that way. I felt stark and thin. I wasn't smiling.

The day was so cold that ice crystals must have formed in my hair by the time I reached the Bakers' front door, and if I hadn't been wearing gloves, my good hand would have lost a chunk of flesh on the wrought-iron door knocker. I rapped it hard. There was a doorbell, too, but chimes would have felt like the wrong music.

Nip and Tuck understood my intentions. When they heard the iron knocker hammering on the pretty yellow door, they must have dashed toward it. I could hear them right on the other side. Rhodesian Ridgebacks were bred to hunt big game and to guard the house. There may be breeds that growl more loudly or deeply than Ridgebacks, but none I've ever heard can growl more menacingly than those African lion hounds. When mastiffs, bullmastiffs, and Rottweilers growl, it fits. They look tough and sound tough. Ridgebacks? They're quiet, peaceful dogs, strong and elegant—except for that blood-chilling contrabass that starts deep in the abdomen, rolls and builds in the throat, and hones itself to sharp thunder as it passes through a Ridgeback's jaws. I'm not afraid of dogs, but at the sound of that roar, my heart traveled back to my chest, where it had room to double in size and pound until my ears rang. And I finally understood the fit between the Bakers and their dogs. Rhodesian Ridgebacks are not always what they seem.

I've never known whether Kelly Baker expected me or not. When she opened the door, she had a hand around Nip's collar, and the big, beautiful dog was glaring at me and still growling softly. Tuck, the bitch, echoed him as she paced nervously behind Kelly.

"Dogs," I said. "I've been thinking a lot about dogs this morning. I've been meditating on the subject of dogs and deceit."

"Come in," she said. "The dogs won't hurt you." The fine skin on her face was even paler than mine, except for the dark purple marks under her eyes. She was wearing a flour-spotted blue denim apron and under it, a light peach jogging suit with stained cuffs.

"I know," I said, and somehow I felt confident that it was true. Even with my stitched and bandaged hand pulsating out proof that a dog would, in fact, bite me, I wasn't afraid of them. I was afraid of her and frightened of confronting her, much more frightened than I'd been of Joel, more frightened than I still was of him.

The front hall, like the kitchen it led to, had the kind of red-brown Welsh tile that my own kitchen linoleum is meant to simulate until I can afford the real thing. A newly refinished Victorian coatrack stood in a corner, with a couple of Kelly's bright parkas suspended from its hooks and a collection of hats and mittens layered on a little shelf at the top. The coatrack dwarfed Kelly, as I did myself, and, as always, the two big, muscular dogs made a dramatic foil for her tiny, conventional femininity. A little table in the hall held out-of-season paper-whites in a delicately painted cachepot. The half-rotten odor of the forced spring flowers mixed weirdly with the wholesome smell of fresh bread.

Kelly pulled Nip toward the kitchen, and Tuck trailed after them, eyeing me as I followed her. An industrial-size mixer equipped with a bread hook stood on one of the cherry counters. White dough coated the hook, and a broad, wide, floured pastry board sat next to the machine. On another cutting board were arrayed four perfect, oversize blood oranges, one already peeled and cut into slices, and a white-handled knife with a narrow, finely serrated, razor-thin blade. A tiny red light glowed on the restaurant range; the oven was on. A futuristic machine that wasn't a Mr. Coffee made dripping sounds and smelled like French roast. Kelly had been cooking a normal breakfast. No, an ideal breakfast. The best coffee. Perfect oranges. Home-baked bread.

"You want to sit down?" Kelly let go of the dog's collar and waved her hand toward a high stool at the granite island in the middle of the kitchen. The dogs had stopped growling, and both lay down on the tile. "I won't offer you anything to eat."

"That's good," I said. "Don't." But I sat on the stool. On the granite in front of me was an array of five-by-eight blue-lined index cards. Embossed in red at the two upper corners of each card were tiny, stylized pictures of flowers, and, between the flowers, also embossed in red, were the words "From the Kitchen of Kelly Baker." One of the cards showed a neatly scripted recipe for raisin pumpernickel bread. Some of the cards were blank. I rested my elbows on the granite and tucked my chin into my good hand. "You got my message," I added.

She edged the oven door open and peered in. Then she turned toward me, let her arms fall helpless to her sides, and started to cry.

"You have to understand that no one does something like this to my dogs," I said. "No one. No one hurts them. You can't do it to them, and you can't do it to me. I don't know why you ever thought you could. And stop crying. Where the hell is Joel?"

She ran a hand over her face and wiped both hands on the apron. "In his office. He's been up all night."

"Doing what?"

"Writing up his cases, every one of them. He says he's referring everyone, and he needs to have something to give to the therapists he refers to. He always does that whenever he makes a referral. He doesn't just hand out names and tell people to try calling."

"How responsible of him," I said.

"It is!" For the first time, she sounded angry. "Most therapists just give people a couple of names. They never even bother to call the therapists to see if they have time or if they're interested."

"He's a perfect little model of ethical conduct, isn't he?" I said.

"He damn well is," she said. "It's no joke."

"I know it's not a joke. A lot of what's happened would sound like some melodramatic joke, but none of it is."

"I feel sick about your dogs."

"I feel sick about Elaine," I said. "I feel sick about Donna Zalewski, and I never even met her."

When she reached toward me, I thought for a second that she was going to grab me, but all she did was pick up the recipe cards and start tapping them until their edges were even.

"Joel didn't do anything," she said. "You of all people know that. Nobody played fair with him."

"Nobody played fair with Kimi, either," I said.

"Who the hell feeds cottage cheese to dogs anymore?"

"A lot of people used to," I said. "Some people still do. You should have known that. When you think about it, it's like Sinequan, isn't it? It isn't trendy, but people still use it, don't they? Is that what it was in the chocolate? For once, you got into some kind of culinary rut? I thought you were supposed to avoid using the same ingredient over and over again. Isn't that one of the basic principles?"

And, of course, she started crying. "I would never, never hurt a dog."

"I played fair before," I said. "I gave Joel twenty-four hours. You know why? Mostly because I felt sorry for both of you, and I also felt sorry for his clients. What Donna and Elaine did to him was totally unfair."

"It could happen to anyone," Kelly said. "Have you thought about that? It could happen to any male therapist, any man at all."

"I know. Only this time, it didn't. It happened to Joel."

"And what were we supposed to do?"

"Go away somewhere? Start over? Come clean?"

"We are not dirty."

"I never said you were. I don't think that."

"How would you like to go somewhere and hide and start over? And spend the rest of your life hoping that no one ever catches you?" Then she looked at the dogs. "And what about them?"

I couldn't follow her. "What about them?" I said. "They wouldn't care."

"We're supposed to vanish somewhere, right? Like criminals? And how were we supposed to show the dogs after that? Just how were we supposed to register them for a show? Our names would be there, in every catalog. And how were we supposed to breed Tuck when we couldn't say who we were? Was she supposed to have puppies that we couldn't register because we didn't dare to write our names down?" Tears were rolling down her face.

As I may have mentioned, I've always admitted that I'm not sane on the subject of dogs. I'd always believed it, too, until I finally got what she meant. Compared with her, I was a paragon of mental health. I believed her, of course, but Rita said later that she wasn't crying about dogs at all. She wasn't crying about not entering Nip and Tuck in AKC shows, but about losing what Rita called "the consensually validated legitimacy" of her life with Joel. And she wasn't crying about puppies, either, according to Rita, but about human babies she couldn't have herself. It's possible that Rita and I are both right about what was really wrong with Kelly Baker. I understood, as most people, including Rita, might not, that her craziness consisted of blurring the distinction between people and dogs.

"The dogs wouldn't have cared if they'd never been to a show again," I said. "All the dogs care about is you, Kelly—you and Joel, and maybe each other. They don't care if Joel wants to pretend to be a man."

When I said that, she stared hard at me and shook her head back and forth in a series of nervous little jerks. "I don't know what you're talking about," she said.

I went on. "Things like that don't fool dogs at all. Kimi wasn't fooled, and your dogs aren't, either. But they don't care. They don't give a damn about superficial things. They want to be fed. They want to be warm. And they want to be with the pack and know where they belong. They are incapable of serious deceit. It never occurs to them to be what they aren't. And they can kill, but they can't commit murder."

"I need to get this bread out of the oven," Kelly said brightly. "The crust is supposed to be crunchy, but Joel just hates it if it's too brown, and I haven't finished slicing the oranges, either."

Before I knew the Bakers, if somebody had asked me, in the abstract, who was more strange, a woman pretending to be a man or the woman married to the first woman, I'd have answered wrong. Of the two, Kelly was by far the weirder.

"Kelly, listen to me. I have tried to be so fair and so sympathetic and such a goddamned perfect liberal that I could have died for it. I know that what started this was nothing more than bad luck. If Donna Zalewski had happened to see some other therapist and not Joel, none of it would've happened. Or if she'd told that story to somebody besides Elaine, somebody who wasn't so happy to believe her. It almost didn't happen. But it did, you know, and it has real consequences. In fact, two women are dead. I can't pretend that didn't happen."

She repeated something she'd said before: "I feel sick about your dogs." Then she added an accusation. "You should have known not to give them chocolate. I shouldn't have trusted you. I'm *so* sorry."

"This discussion is not rational," I said, mostly to myself. "And I can't take it much more. We are talking about people, not dogs. I'm going to get Joel, and the three of us are calling the police. I have had all I can stand of all this damned ambiguity about everything. We're going to get it all out in the open. I don't know what else to do."

"I do." Her tone was pert and superior. "You're just like everybody else, aren't you? I know what you think of me. Everybody thinks I'm the most reactionary woman in Cambridge." Pride filled her voice. "But I have a lot of clever ideas. You'd be surprised."

"I'm sure you're clever," I said. "I wouldn't be surprised at all."

"Go and get Joel," she ordered me, as if she wanted me to do nothing more than summon him to breakfast, and, in fact, she picked up the white-handled knife and began pulling the peel off an orange.

When I got down from the high stool, the scraping of its legs on the hard tile disturbed the dogs, who escorted me silently to the front hallway. There was certainly an inside staircase that led down to Joel's office, but I didn't want to poke around looking for it, and I didn't want to ask Kelly for directions. I felt guilty for letting Kelly continue to believe that she'd killed Kimi and Rowdy, and I almost turned back to tell her that they were alive. I also felt guilty about Nip and Tuck, whose pack was about to disintegrate. They weren't growling, and I could probably have patted them both, but I didn't. It would have been a sleazy thing to do, a superficial gesture of unfounded reassurance. I let myself out and followed the little brick path around the house. The temperature outside had risen to about zero.

The door to Joel's office was locked. I couldn't find a doorbell, and I had to tap on the glass for a long time before he appeared. As usual, he had on a suit, but his tie was loose, and his shirt was unbuttoned at the top. He looked tired and distracted.

"Come with me," I said.

"Just give me five minutes. I'm almost done. I canceled all my appointments last night, and I've only got one more client to finish writing up. I just hope everybody takes these referrals."

I followed him down the stairs to his waiting room.

"Kelly is in bad shape," I said.

"Five minutes. I need to finish this. I need to know it's done."

"She's acting very weird."

"That's what happens when denial breaks down," he said.

"We have to get this over now. I know I told you twenty-four hours, but that was before. Didn't you understand my message? Kelly did."

"I've been here all night," he said. "She's only been down a couple of times."

"I left a message on your machine."

"Here or home?"

"The one to call for emergencies. Home, I guess."

"It's upstairs," he said. "I haven't checked it. Oh, Christ. I hope none of my clients called."

"Joel, wake up. It's a lot worse than that. When I left here yesterday, Kelly handed me a package of chocolate croissants. After I got home, my dogs stole the package, and they got a lot sicker than if they'd just eaten chocolate. A whole lot worse. I left a message that I couldn't wake them up. Kelly didn't tell you?"

He gave a big, pained sigh. "Your beautiful dogs."

"They'll be all right," I said. "They survived. But it was very close."

"Does Kelly know they're all right?"

"No," I said. "Come on. She's acting strange."

He opened a door in the waiting room and took quick, familiar steps up a flight of beige-carpeted stairs. By the time I got to the little hallway at the top, he was on the other side of what turned out to be a back door to the kitchen. He didn't close it, but when I tried to follow him in, Tuck blocked my way. Her strong legs were braced, and her growl warned me not to push past her. When I heard Joel's voice, I thought he must be talking to a dog, presumably to Nip. He was murmuring, but I couldn't make out the words, and I couldn't see either him or Kelly.

"Joel? Tuck won't let me in," I called. "Kelly? Call the dog, would you?"

I heard a soft thump of something on that hard floor, then Joel appeared. The front of his shirt was stained with blood. "Tuck," he said quietly. "Tuck, here."

The Ridgeback stopped growling at me, and I opened the door wide. I waited for Joel to speak, but he only stared vacantly at me. His face was empty, completely without expression, as if the person inside had left.

"Joel?"

"She used a Sheffield knife," he said blankly. "She didn't have much time. I guess she didn't have much choice."

"Where's Nip?"

Joel pointed with his chin. "Back there. Did you think . . . ? You didn't know her very well, did you? Kelly would never hurt a dog."

Chapter 25

"LET me see her." I must have sounded ghoulish, but it's hard to tell whether a creature—a person or another animal—is dead. When in doubt, assume life.

Kelly Baker, though, sprawled on the tile near the granite island, had made a gory mess of leaving little room for doubt. She'd taken off the apron and plunged the white-handled knife into her chest, the same narrow-bladed knife she'd been using to peel and slice the blood oranges. The juice and zest must still have been clinging to the blade when she turned it on herself. I knelt down beside her.

"Joel, get the dogs away. And call someone." For once, I wanted no dogs around.

The Ridgebacks were not, of course, trying to drink her blood, and they weren't licking her. Nip, in fact, was asleep in a corner of the room. Dogdom's champion dozers, Rhodesian Ridgebacks guard their slumber as if it's a diamond mine they've been trained to keep inviolate. Neither Kelly's suicide nor our voices had broken through Nip's defenses, but Tuck was wide awake and nervous, pacing around and whipping her tail back and forth.

"Joel, call someone," I repeated. "For Christ's sake, get the dogs out and call someone. Or I will."

I sat on the cold tile next to Kelly and picked up her tiny, limp left hand. I tried to find a pulse, but I'm not sure I know how. I couldn't feel or see a sign of life, but I kept holding her hand while Joel put the dogs in another room and used the phone. It must take extraordinary control to do psychotherapy and even greater control to spend your whole adult life passing yourself off as someone you're not—or to keep passing yourself off as someone you've become, someone who isn't the person you once were. Joel's voice didn't crack or give out on him. He sounded exactly the same as always. "It's the pale yellow house with the fenced yard," he said calmly and slowly. I heard him hang up. He wandered to the massive doors of the refrigerator and freezer, only a few yards from where Kelly lay, and faced the appliance doors as if to study the inventories.

"She left a note," he said, as if remarking that she had made a shopping list or had run to the store and would be right back. Still facing away from me, he held up one of her recipe cards.

Hysteria filled my chest and bottlenecked in my throat. When I dropped her hand, it hit the tile with a soft splat. From the Kitchen of Kelly Baker. Waves of hideous laughter pressed the back of my tongue and gagged me. No other element had seemed so grotesque, or maybe Kelly had compressed all of the grotesquerie onto a five-by-eight recipe card. Elaine, to whom a life of exclusive domesticity meant a living death, would have interpreted the symbolism, I thought. I began to sober up.

"Joel? What did she write?"

He remained silent.

"Did she make a confession?"

"Of sorts," he said. "She confessed to depression. To infertility." He turned to face me and leaned the back of his head against the freezer door. His eyes moved back and forth as if searching the ceiling for cobwebs. "I wanted to leave. I wanted to go anywhere. She refused. She cared much more than I did. In a way, she was like those tiny women who get a kind of superhuman strength in a crisis, a rush of adrenaline. Those women who lift up cars when their children are trapped underneath?" For the first time that I'd seen, he looked down at her body. "Or more like someone who steps in front of a speeding car to stop it from killing someone else." He paused and then added, to himself, it seemed: "She had more investment in my identity than I do myself."

Marriage does that to women, Elaine would have said.

Kelly was dead, of course. She knew how to use a kitchen knife. When the ambulance took her body, Joel went, too. I said nothing to anyone about anything except to confirm that

Kelly had stabbed herself and that she had told me how desperate she was for a baby.

If the weather had been warmer, I'd have taken the Ridgebacks home with me and boarded them in my yard, but zero degrees with no doghouse would have been cruel. With Joel and Kelly gone, the dogs were glad to follow anyone willing to take charge of them. Without any tugging on their leashes, I led them to the Bronco, and they soared into the back. When I got to Steve's, he was in surgery, but Rhonda, one of his aides, took the dogs. I collected Rowdy and drove home. With my bandaged hand encased in a plastic bag, I took one of those prolonged, boiling showers that scald fragile skin. It left me red-splotched and woozy. I put on a flannel nightgown printed all over with flowers, unplugged the phone, got into bed, and picked up the new L. L. Bean catalog that was on the nightstand. Rowdy wandered around the bedroom looking mystified and disoriented. I'm not a daytime napper. And where was Kimi?

"Bed," I told him. I thumped the comforter with my good hand. One of the luxuries of owning a highly intelligent dog is the freedom to declare exceptions to rules. Let a stupid dog sleep on the bed only once, and you'll have to keep kicking him off for the rest of his life, but an Alaskan malamute can understand that something is forbidden unless you give permission. Rowdy made a long, happy arc in the air and landed next to me. "Good boy," I told him.

A good grip on a dog is a grip on reality. With an arm wrapped around Rowdy's sturdy, furry neck, I studied the most comforting prose in the English language, that great refuge from uncertainty, the fully fashioned, practical, durable world of L. L. Bean, where the well-constructed pants are always cut full through the hips and thighs to provide unrestricted mobility, and turtlenecks of breathable knit neither bind nor bag. All sleeves are designed to allow freedom of arm and shoulder movement. Sweaters create a richly textured, intricate appearance, and shirts retain their crisp, fresh look. It is a prewashed, preshrunk land reliably bar-tacked at points of stress, a land devoid of difficult personal decisions: Lightweight jackets provide warmth and wind resistance on brisk fall and spring days. Utility jackets are appropriate for errands, shopping, and weekend yard work at home. All products are guaranteed to give 100% satisfaction in every way. Nothing is ambiguous, and you never have to think for yourself. I fell asleep.

A stupid or selfish dog would have awakened me at his dinnertime. Rowdy let me sleep until nine that night, when he planted his wet nose on my cheek. Then he let loose a series of snarls that sounded like an immediate threat to rip my throat open. Translated from the malamute, it was a polite request to go out.

Not long after I let him into the fenced yard and back into the house, and fed him dinner, Rita came home early from a date and tapped on the kitchen door. Her hair was swept away from her face and smelled of hair spray, and she was wearing a mauve silk dress and lots of silver jewelry. While I put on jeans and a sweatshirt, she scrambled two eggs and made toast for me. I told her what had happened and how, oddly, I'd slept. Therapists are more interested in responses to events than in events themselves.

"Regression in the service of the ego," Rita said. "It's a useful defense. There's nothing wrong with it."

"If Rowdy hadn't been frantic to be let out, I might've slept until morning. I never sleep in the daytime. And this was some strange kind of heavy, drugged sleep. The food is helping. I think I might've eaten lunch yesterday, but I'm not sure. I'm not really awake yet."

"So what's that about? That heavy sleep?"

"I was tired." That kind of answer never satisfies Rita.

"Of . . . ?"

"Complexity. Ambiguity. You know what I want?"

"A dog," she said.

I laughed. It felt like the first time in years. "No. For once."

"So what do you want?"

"One answer, just one. I'm tired of everything being complicated. I want one reason for everything. I want some kind of clarity."

"That's not what's bothering you," she said.

"I killed her. I think I meant to do it."

"And how did you accomplish it?"

Anybody else, except maybe another therapist, would have assured me that I was innocent.

"By not telling her about the dogs. I let her think she'd killed them. I could have told her they were all right, but I didn't. I let her think she'd killed them. I did it deliberately. I mean, I didn't say to myself, 'Well, if I don't tell her they're okay, if I let her think they died, then she'll kill herself.' But I did want her to suffer for it. I wanted revenge. And she really did try to kill me."

"I believe you," Rita said.

"And Kimi almost died. That's what I wanted to kill her for. In a way, I'm not that different from Kelly. Actually, what I did was worse. She was protecting someone, and I wasn't. I knew Kimi was okay. And I didn't do it because of Donna and Elaine, either. I did it because of my dogs. I wanted revenge. It doesn't feel very good now that I've got it."

"I can see that," Rita said.

"And it's partly because I was so devious. And what came to me in a kind of flash, after I'd been trying to work everything out but really just delaying and putting things off, is that if I'd been dealing with men, I wouldn't have done that. I wouldn't have hesitated. But even after I realized that, it didn't really change things. I still wasn't direct."

"Insight doesn't automatically change behavior, you know."

"Well, it seems as if it should. I mean, what was it I got all of a sudden? First, that I'm more afraid of women that I am of men, but, second, I also have this image of us, that we aren't fair game."

"Or," Rita said gently, "this is a world that makes it difficult for women to act directly, and people prevented from acting directly become people who find it difficult to play fair."

"That's very charitable."

"Do you have anything to drink? I can run upstairs."

"There's some of Kevin's Budweiser, or you can have Scotch."

"Scotch."

"Water?"

"Just ice."

I dropped the cubes into a glass tumbler that Rowdy won at a fun match, filled it three-quarters full, and handed it to her.

"Thanks," she said.

"You know what? Have you ever seen those old movies where at the end, you find out that some guy murdered someone? And he's about to be arrested, but then some suave English guy tells him he's got the chance to take the honorable way out. So he goes into his wood-paneled study, and you see the door close on him, and you hear a gunshot. Right? He's done the honorable thing. Well, you know what? It's not like that."

"There are other ways to think about this." She made it sound like a statement of fact, not an accusation.

"Such as?"

"That the effort to sustain the illusion became too much for her. For all these years, she'd been living as if things were true that just plain were not. And that's not your responsibility. You might also want to consider the possibility that all the things she did really had very little connection with any secret about Joel."

"Bullshit, Rita. They had everything to do with it."

"Not necessarily. In a way, maybe she reaped the consequences of making someone else the center of her own life."

"Would you not make some sickening feminist parable out of it? You sound like Elaine."

"So what?"

"Okay. So what," I said. "I liked Elaine more than you did. So Kelly made someone else the center of her life."

"And maybe it doesn't make any difference who that someone is."

"It does," I said. "It makes a difference if the center of your life is keeping up some kind of pretense. I mean, if what's at the center is fake. Not Joel. The whole illusion."

"It reminds me of something Gloria Steinem said." Rita stretched her arms, rolled her neck a little, and then held still. "You know what she said about Marilyn Monroe? She said, 'Marilyn Monroe was a female impersonator. We're all female impersonators.' "

"Joel isn't. But, okay, I get it. Kelly was even more than most of us, right? Joel sort of said the same thing. So okay. She was more of an impersonator than he is. And to begin with, Donna Zalewski, of course. That abuse act was another kind of impersonation, you know? Playing the role of the victim."

Rita shook her head.

"No?"

"Holly, ask yourself: How would someone happen to select that role?"

"Oh, God."

"With a patient like that, a woman? A woman with those symptoms? Always. People never lie, Holly. All they do is alter the details."

"Her father?"

"My supposition is an uncle who lived with the family off and on. We never dealt with it directly. I didn't have time to see her, and I didn't want it surfacing in what had to be a brief contact. My hunch is that what happened with Joel is that it did start to surface, before their alliance was strong enough to withstand it, and she ran scared."

"She didn't actually tell you?"

"She probably didn't remember."

"But how could anyone forget . . . ?"

"Sometimes the only survival option is to pretend it didn't happen," Rita said. "And to some extent, it works for a while. The defenses people use always represent the best they can do at the time. How is anyone supposed to anticipate the long-term consequences? Is a child supposed to stop and realize that pretense distorts all relationships, relationships with oneself and with other people? You wanted one answer? That's it. Anatomy doesn't matter, but relationships do. That's the only thing that matters, the quality of relationships. One answer."

Chapter 26

Kevin's Budweiser sat untouched in my refrigerator for a couple of weeks, but I threw out his plastic-wrapped hamburger when it turned brownish purple and grew a sheen of slime, and I tossed the white-and-blue-spotted sandwich buns into the yard for the birds and squirrels. He made me go to the Central Square Station twice. When he finally stopped in at my house, he insisted on talking in the living room, not the kitchen, even though the living room radiator is always turned off unless I'm expecting company, and after it's turned on, it usually takes at least an hour to heat the room.

"Let me get this straight," he said for maybe the tenth time.

We were sitting on opposite ends of the couch. Until I can afford the pair of soft chairs that are going to flank the fireplace, the only place to sit, besides on the couch, is the floor. I don't like junk, and junk is what the old chairs were. The floor would've been even colder than the couch. Also, neither of us wanted to be one down.

"I am freezing," I said.

"Get a sweater."

"This is stupid. Can't we just forget that this is an official visit and hang out in the kitchen where it's warm?"

"So he ran up the stairs ahead of you."

"Yes."

"He entered the kitchen first. You attempted to enter, but the dog barked at you. You stopped."

"Yes."

"And since when was it that you suddenly got so afraid of dogs?"

"Kevin, she meant business. She wasn't barking. She was

172

growling, and her whole posture was something I didn't want to fool around with. And remember? I already had one bite. I didn't need another." I displayed my hand. The bandage was off, and the stitches were out, but the scars showed.

"And how was it that that happened?"

"She just bit me. That's all. It was my own fault. She isn't vicious. I was careless."

"Okay. So he enters the kitchen. How far behind him are you?"

"Not far."

"Let's try it again. When you get there, is the door open?"

"Ajar. I've already told you that."

"And how many minutes ahead of you is he?"

"Seconds. I don't know. I got there a few seconds after he did. Ten seconds, okay?"

"And when you opened the door, did you see him?"

"I didn't look. I'm telling you, I looked at the dog."

"Christ."

"Well, I wasn't stopping to admire her."

"And how long was it you stood looking at the dog?"

"I have no idea."

"An hour."

"Of course not. A few seconds. I have no idea. Then I must've looked up. I called to Joel and Kelly to get Tuck. But I didn't see anyone because he must've been kneeling down beside her. She was on the opposite side of that kitchen island, on the opposite side from where I was. And he was, too."

"And when you left the kitchen before, the knife was on a cutting board."

"No, it was not. It was in her hand. She was peeling and slicing oranges. This was a boring conversation the first time we had it, and it isn't getting more interesting. If you'd just spit out what you're after, I'd tell you if I knew, and we could go into the kitchen and warm up."

Kevin's frankness is one of his winning qualities. "To tell you the God's honest truth, I'm not a hundred percent sure."

"Fine, then I'll tell you. You want to know if he had time to stab her. He did not. Furthermore, she left a suicide note. If she made any noise, we didn't hear it because his office suite is totally soundproof, just like every other therapy office. Ask Rita. What more do you want?"

He put one hand in the other, spread his elbows, and flexed his shoulder muscles. "I hate discrepancies. They eat at me."

"I don't see any."

"Here we have an attractive woman with a successful husband." Elaine wouldn't have let him get away with that. "He makes a lot of money. They live in a nice house in a nice neighborhood. Two new cars. No bills. She's got hobbies. Dogs. Cooking. And all of a sudden, she has a brainstorm. She picks up a knife and does herself in because she's infertile, quote unquote."

"That can be terrible for people. It's easy for other people to dismiss it and say they should adopt, but some couples have a terrible time about it. It can make people very depressed, especially if they blame themselves."

"She's infertile, right? The body shows no evidence of semen. That's what's missing from the picture. You know? Like those games in kids' magazines. And now, boys and girls, see if you can find what's missing from this picture. And what's missing is sperm."

"You must've read some very strange magazines when you were a kid."

He didn't even smile. "She was ovulating. A woman commits suicide because she's infertile. What's wrong with this picture? She's ovulating, and there's no trace of seminal fluid."

"She didn't necessarily know she was ovulating. Maybe she thought she wasn't, and they were waiting until she was. People do that."

"You know, Holly, there's something about that guy I just don't like."

"He has a lot of self-control. He's grieving for his wife. He's probably blaming himself, angry at her and a lot of other stuff. Suicide is very hard on the survivors. He can't exactly be at his best right now."

Kevin shook his big head. "Didn't like him before. Took one look, and something didn't ring right."

"I didn't know you knew him before."

"Your friend Elaine Walsh wrote him a couple of letters."

I don't know why I ever thought the police wouldn't know to examine a hard drive. Of course they'd have seen those letters.

"Oh," I said casually.

"About Donna Zalewski."

"Really?"

"But it didn't pan out. It seems they had some kind of dispute about money."

"Money?"

"What they call third-party payments. She had insurance, Blue Cross, and Walsh thought Baker was bilking her and the insurance company."

"How was that?"

"Baker told me all about it. Double-billing, they call it. These guys have to register with Blue Cross." (Rita, for instance, is a guy who's a Blue Cross provider, but Kevin would have resented my charging him with sexism.) He continued: "And they have to sign something that says they'll only charge so much. And maybe then they get greedy and decide it's not enough, so they get their patients to pay a little extra something on the side. Or maybe they don't want to wait for the insurance company to pay up, and they make the patients pay on the spot, and then when they get the insurance check, maybe they hold on to it awhile and collect the interest."

"Did Joel Baker do that?"

"Naw. Like I told you, it didn't pan out. One of the guys went through it all with him. One of the ID numbers on a form had a couple of digits reversed, and Blue Cross held up the payment, and then paid up slow. They verified the whole thing. It didn't pan out."

The autopsy finding still bothers Kevin, but it doesn't bother anyone else I know because autopsy reports are confidential medical records. But two points he made worried me a little. Rita reassured me about the first one. She said that mix-ups with insurance payments happen all the time and that insurance companies always take a long time to pay. Joel Baker had been slightly lucky to have that explanation available, but only slightly.

Kevin's persistent questions about whether Joel had had time to murder Kelly bothered me because, of course, I never had any definite, concrete proof that Kelly, not Joel, had murdered Donna and Elaine. When Joel told me that he'd been willing to disappear and start over somewhere else, I believed him, and I believed that Kelly hadn't been willing to leave. She knew who Dr. Arsenault was, and she could have gone to him just as I'd done. Joel could have, too, but I believed that he genuinely despised Arsenault and wouldn't have gone to him under any circumstances. It would have been hard for Joel, easy for Kelly to doctor their own cottage cheese and substitute it for Elaine's. I also trusted Rita's good opinion of Joel. I trusted my own.

Then one day when I pulled the Bronco into my driveway, Joel was right there on Appleton Street, walking Nip and Tuck. He'd taken over the task since Kelly's death, I'd noticed. I'd seen him with the dogs quite a few times, but I'd always been in the car or far away, and I hadn't spoken to him. Kelly had always kept Tuck, the bitch, on lead, but she usually hadn't leashed Nip, who didn't stray far enough to worry her. Joel had them both leashed. If they missed Kelly, their grief wasn't marring their appearance, and although Joel probably didn't do the marathon dog-walking Kelly had done, the Ridgebacks still looked sleek, muscular, and fit.

The dogs didn't growl at me when I got out of the car. In fact, they brightened up and headed toward me. Joel followed. I let Nip and Tuck sniff my hands before I patted them. Joel looked just as he had when Kelly was alive, as if he'd just had a shave and haircut. He wore a camel's-hair coat that didn't show wheaten Ridgeback fur, and on his hands were heavy, masculine brown leather gloves. I told him that he and the dogs were looking well, and I sat on the back steps to be at dog level while I ran my mittens over the Ridgebacks' glossy coats.

While Joel was explaining that he hadn't been showing the dogs, Tuck was whipping her tail back and forth and smiling at me, but Nip lost interest and began to nose at the lid of the milk box. Then he nosed it open. I speak dog, of course. I understood. The day Kelly stood at Elaine's door and opened the milk box, identical to mine and every other Pleasant Valley delivery box, Nip was her excuse in case anyone asked what she was doing there. If anyone asked, she was retrieving her dog. Joel kept both dogs on lead. Only Kelly let Nip wander. In nosing open the box, Nip was showing me what Kelly had done, or maybe even what he'd done for her. Kelly, he told me, Kelly, not Joel.

*   *   *

According to Rita, the rumors about Joel Baker, the ones Sheila Moss had been quietly passing along, have disappeared, and he's getting more referrals than ever. Everyone agrees that he's wonderful with women clients because he's so sympathetic. People say that the source of his strength with couples is his almost uncanny grasp of the viewpoints of both husband and wife. In fact, I ran into Sheila Moss at the Fishmonger the other day. She told me that she wasn't on Prozac anymore, but that she'd felt terrific ever since she and Ben had started seeing Joel Baker. Rita was upset when I told her that. She was more surprised that he'd ignored the boundary between friends and clients than that he'd crossed the boundary between women and men.

People understand that Kelly's suicide has left Joel wary of involvements with women, but practically everyone hopes he'll at least begin to test out some kind of new relationship soon. Rita told me that a few people have been wondering aloud whether he's finally going to come out of the closet.

And my own mind is unmuddled. Rita made everything clear. Freud thought that anatomy is destiny, she said, but he was wrong. Then I understood. The breed of dog doesn't matter. Most goldens retrieve. And obey. Malamutes pull. And obey themselves. But suppose I get the one Alaskan malamute that acts like a golden. He has no interest in pulling a sled and keeps taking things in his mouth and dropping them in front of me. If I insist on harnessing him and making him pull because I'm ashamed of the way he really is, all I do is ruin our relationship. And if I tint his coat yellow-red and try to pass him off as a golden, he senses that I'm ashamed of him, and I let deceit ruin our relationship with each other and with everyone else.

But suppose I say to him, "Well, you are a strange malamute, aren't you? But so what?" His difference is a big plus if I don't fight it and don't try to pretend it isn't there. He gets his C.D. in three straight shows with three perfect scores, then his C.D.X., then his U.D., and eventually, he's that contradiction in terms, an Obedience Trial Champion Alaskan malamute. We're proud of ourselves and each other, and everyone wants to know the secret of our success. The secret is that we didn't create one.

When I explained it to Steve, he said, "Did Rita really say that?"

"That's what she meant," I said, although the literal truth is that she accused me of trivializing things. She was wrong. Dogs are incapable of sustained pretense, and their superhuman incapacity is not trivial.

"Of course," I added, "dogs don't have any choice about what breed they look like, but what if they did? If Joel feels like a man, acts like a man, and all but is a man, why should he pretend to be a woman? That would be deceitful. And was he supposed to have his wife arrested for murder? Was he supposed to betray her like that?"

"Holly, for God's sake," Steve said. "Okay, so breed doesn't matter all that much. What counts is the right dog for the right person. But bitches are bitches, and dogs are dogs. You've been in Cambridge too long. Why don't you go home to Maine for a week or two?"

"I can't. Kimi starts with the beginners this Thursday. Remember Kimi? She's the bitch who lifts her leg."

"That's perfectly normal, especially for a malamute. It's a matter of dominance. It isn't a function of gender."

"Anatomy isn't destiny, you see? What counts is the quality of relationships."

"Go home to Maine. Then come back. We'll work on a quality relationship. Come back and marry me."

I can't possibly get married. The only things I know how to cook right are liver treats and homemade dog biscuits, and I won't waste nine months producing one furless creature doomed to run away from home. Married couples always take their conflicts out on their dogs. My house is too small for Steve's dogs and mine, and with four dogs living here, how could I get another one? And Rowdy would hate living over the clinic. Kimi would undo all the progress Steve has made with Lady. Suppose I brought home an Akita, and Steve objected? Of course, Rowdy and Kimi would protest, but that's different. I'm the alpha wolf in our pack. And, as things are now, Steve is the alpha in his pack. If we merged packs, one of us would lose because a wolf pack never has two alphas. That's what's wrong with marriage.

I'll never get married. When I want to bring home an Akita,

I will. If I ever finish mourning Vinnie, I'll get another golden retriever. I'll always have Alaskan malamutes, of course. In my lifetime, I'll have dozens of them. And after I finally merge with the great celestial pack, I'll come back every now and then. I won't stay long, and I won't pretend to be someone I'm not. If you ever go to an AKC obedience trial and see an Alaskan malamute earning a perfect score in Utility B, you'll know who's there, too, heeling precisely, perfectly at home with herself, home at last.

About the Author

Susan Conant graduated *summa cum laude* from Radcliffe College and holds a doctorate from the Harvard Graduate School of Education. She and her husband live in Newton, Massachusetts, with two cats and two Alaskan malamutes. She trains with the New England and the Charles River Dog Training Clubs. She is happiest with a mystery in her hands and a dog at her feet.

EARLENE FOWLER

introduces Benni Harper, curator of San Celina's folk
art museum and amateur sleuth

__FOOL'S PUZZLE   0-425-14545-X/$6.50

Ex-cowgirl Benni Harper moved to San Celina, California, to begin
a new career as curator of the town's folk art museum. But when one
of the museum's first quilt exhibit artists is found dead, Benni must
piece together a pattern of family secrets and small-town lies to catch
the killer.

__IRISH CHAIN   0-425-15137-9/$6.50

When Brady O'Hara and his former girlfriend are murdered at the San
Celina Senior Citizen's Prom, Benni believes it's more than mere
jealousy. She risks everything—her exhibit, her romance with police
chief Gabriel Ortiz, and her life—to unveil the conspiracy O'Hara had
been hiding for fifty years.

__KANSAS TROUBLES   0-425-15696-6/$5.99

After their wedding, Benni and Gabe visit his hometown near Wichita.
There Benni meets Tyler Brown: aspiring country singer, gifted quilter,
and former Amish wife. But when Tyler is murdered and the case comes
between Gabe and her, Benni learns that her marriage is much like the
Kansas weather: unexpected and bound to be stormy.

Prices slightly higher in Canada

Penguin Putnam Inc.   Bill my: ☐ Visa ☐ MasterCard ☐ Amex _____ (expires)
P.O. Box 12289, Dept. B   Card#_____
Newark, NJ 07101-5289
Please allow 4-6 weeks for delivery.   Signature_____
Foreign and Canadian delivery 6-8 weeks.

Bill to:

Name_____
Address_____ City_____
State/ZIP_____
Daytime Phone #_____

Ship to:

Name_____ Book Total $_____
Address_____ Applicable Sales Tax $_____
City_____ Postage & Handling $_____
State/ZIP_____ Total Amount Due $_____

This offer subject to change without notice.